KOKOPELLi & COMPANY

in

Attack of the SMART PIES

KOKOPELLI & COMPANY

in Attack of the SMART PIES

Larry Gonick

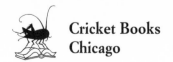

Cricket Books
Chicago

Library of Congress Cataloging-in-Publication Data

Gonick, Larry.
    Attack of the Smart Pies / Larry Gonick.—1st ed.
        p. cm.
    Summary: Feather, one of the "New Muses" who provide humans
with inspiration, reluctantly helps Kokopelli to aim giant, self-guided
pies at Urania while trying to help an orphan girl find some answers
about her family.
    ISBN 0-8126-2740-7
    [1. Helpfulness—Fiction. 2. Tricks—Fiction. 3. Orphans—Fiction.
4. Runaways—Fiction. 5. Humorous stories.] I. Title.
    PZ7.G58725At 2005
    [Fic]—dc22
                            2004021253

For Sophie and Anna and Gabriel

1

Are Doughnuts a Vegetable?

FEATHER WOULD NEVER have gone to the mall, except for the doughnuts. If not for the doughnuts, he would have stayed home. This was because Feather was a Muse, and Muses try to keep clear of Human Beings as much as possible. Humans can be so rude. They have a strange way of opening their mouths wide when they see you. They gasp out loud and stare at you and drop their packages, if they have packages. You would think they had never seen anyone with a broad orange beak, feathered headdress, fringed overcoat, or oversized wings before.

To be fair, thought Feather, not all Humans lacked manners. There were a few faces in the crowd without bulging eyes or gaping mouths. Some looked perfectly normal. Others avoided his eyes. Still others trembled with suppressed amazement, laughter, or even fear, but managed to keep themselves under control. And one face gazed at him calmly, with frank curiosity: a child's face framed by tangled, curly dark hair, a small, sad face that quickly turned away when he met its eyes.

Meanwhile, all around him, packages were falling to the floor with a thud or a crunch (That one sounded like a set of dishes, thought Feather with something like satisfaction), and people were muttering and nudging their friends. "Why do I put up with this?" he asked himself, and his stomach growled back the answer: for the doughnuts.

Feather was a strict vegetarian, but sometimes he craved a change from his sensible diet of steamed vegetables, tofu, and brown rice. To put it plainly, he craved doughnuts—aren't doughnuts a vegetable?—and doughnuts were found at the mall. So, with clenched beak, he waited in line outside the Krusty-Glop DoNut Shop at the Great Buy and Buy, a sprawling mall complex at the intersection of Anonymous Road and Generic Highway.

The line was long. If Feather craned his neck, he could see it snaking far ahead into the distance, past Starbucks, Video Villa, Pizza Pit, Pretzel Pavilion, Origami Barn, and another Starbucks, before finally entering the far-off door to Krusty-Glop. At the moment he was standing outside Gender Gap, a store that, despite its name, sold trendy clothes.

Even at this distance, Feather could smell doughnuts. And what a smell! It was enough to cloud the mind of even a strong-minded Muse, and Feather was anything but strong-minded. How, he wondered idly, did Krusty-Glop produce that perfect combination of maple, vanilla, and chocolate, with a hint of raspberries and plum? And how did they spread it over the neighborhood? Was it their recipes, or  was it, just possibly, some special bricks? Bricks with millions of little holes that let the doughnuts' sugary essence seep through to the outside air . . .

He imagined acres of glistening pastries, vast trays of them rolling out of the kitchen, fresh from their bath of hot fat—Kranberry Krullers, oozing yellowish, custardy, berry-studded goop and exuding that glorious whiff of fried dough and burnt sugar . . . Pumpkin Puffs, so very . . . plump . . . and Sinful Cinnamons, so extremely . . . round . . . His head swam. Should he order a dozen all alike or a mixed lot? Or two dozen and save some for later? Even stale doughnuts were better than fresh broccoli. He stood paralyzed, licking his lips, or rather the rim of his beak.

"Long line," said a voice over his shoulder.

Feather ignored it. He had never known a Human to make small talk with a Muse. The voice must be speaking to someone else.

He felt a sharp poke between the shoulder blades, just above his wings.

"I *said,* long line," repeated the voice.

Feather wheeled around. Behind him stood a girl about twelve years old. She had curly, tousled, dark hair and a sad, though slightly *assertive,* expression. Strange . . . it was the same face he had seen earlier in the crowd. She had just given him a hard nudge in the back, and now she wanted to *talk?* Feather felt a rising sense of panic.

"Is this a Halloween costume?" asked the girl. She was actually fingering the fringes on his robe! Stop it! "Because if it is, you should know that Halloween was months ago."

"Uh . . . ah . . . er . . . it's not a Halloween costume," mumbled Feather under his breath.

"Hm? Are you a superhero?" Her large brown eyes looked at him intently, as if his answer meant the world to her. This was bad. She was much too interested. Feather wished he knew how to lie, but he was always terribly truthful. He decided to say as little as possible.

"No."

Her face brightened. "You're an alien, aren't you?"

Feather groaned. Why wouldn't she leave him *alone?* He wanted to flee, but that would have meant giving up *doughnuts.* His stomach whimpered like a lonely puppy.

"You don't have to answer that," hissed the girl in his ear. "I can tell you're something special. Something more than human. So I wonder . . . please . . . can you help me?"

The word *help* works magic on a Muse. Muses live to help. Feather relaxed a little.

"What kind of help do you need?" he whispered, trying to keep their conversation from anyone else's ears.

"It's hard to explain in a minute or two. Can we go somewhere else to talk?"

Feather thought long and hard about doughnuts.

"That depends," he replied at last. "What kind of problem is it? Is it about plants?" Plants were Feather's second-favorite subject, after doughnuts.

"No . . . not really . . . it's more of a family problem. Something has happened . . . and I'm scared—"

She was interrupted by the sound of falling packages. This could mean only one thing: another Muse was at the mall. Feather cocked his head and listened. The crashing sounded muffled. It seemed to be coming from inside a nearby store—in fact, just beyond the display window beside him. Feather leaned his face against the glass and peered in.

He saw a tall, angular female figure with a triangular head and triangular ears and four elongated triangular spikes of—was it hair? feathers? a bizarre hat? Feather was never sure—rising from her forehead. This was Mimi, the Muse of Getting Along with People. Mimi was the only Muse who really liked the mall, because she loved to shop, though it was hard to understand why. Nothing she tried on ever fit. Just look at her shape. Even her torso was triangular, tapering to a waist barely four inches around. Her arms and legs were like sticks.

She was holding a T-shirt up to her shoulders. Of course, it was much too wide at the waist.

Feather felt a jab in his ribs. Luckily, he was well padded, because these fingers were sharp.

"I asked you a question," said the curly-headed girl testily. "Can you help me?"

Feather shrugged. "I'm terribly sorry," he said. The

girl scowled. "But," he went on, "there's someone in the store who may be able to help. She understands Humans much better than I do."

Just as the girl pressed her face against the glass, more packages crashed somewhere off to their left. There was a murmur, a commotion, a stir. Feather turned. A majestic female figure in a long, gray dress swept through the crowd. Her blond head was held high, and the red ribbons that bound her hair streamed behind her. She drew a great, lavender cloak tightly around herself, as a shield against the lowly masses. This was Urania, Muse of Astronomy, who *never* mingled with Humans. Odd . . .

"Have you seen Mimi?" she asked Feather in a voice as icy as the winds of outer space. He pointed inside.

Urania entered the Gender Gap (that was the name of the store, you may recall) and began a whispered conversation with Mimi. Feather and the girl beside him peered in, following every move. At first, Mimi tried to ignore the Astronomy Muse and concentrate on shirts, but after much talk from Urania, Mimi finally looked at her. They exchanged a few more words. Mimi backed away nervously from Urania. Urania tried to approach her.

"Get away from me!" Mimi shrieked.

Mimi ran out of the store, with Urania hard on her heels. They almost collided with Feather. "Wait, Mimi!" said Urania. "You can help—"

"Look out!" screamed Mimi. "Look out for the pies

from the skies!" She charged straight at a crowd of by-standers, who stood aside to let her pass, and she was gone.

"Was that the one who could help me?" the girl asked Feather pointedly.

"I'm afraid so," he said with a sigh.

Feather heard a whooshing, whistling sound. The girl looked into the sky. She pushed Feather in front of Urania.

Feather felt a hard, wet *smack* on his face. Then a burning sensation. Was it hot or cold? Cold, he decided. And why couldn't he *see?* He tried to open his mouth, but it seemed to be glued shut. Something, appar-ently, was stuck to his face. He raised his  hands and felt—what? His fingers sank into a cold, sticky, pastelike material . . . sticky and fluffy and lumpy . . . and sweet, he could taste it now, sweet in a yucky way, like artificial bananas . . . and some crumbly hard bits, too . . . and on top of everything, a lightweight, metallic plate, which came loose and clattered to the floor.

"I'm sorry, Feather," said Urania, sounding very far away. "I think that was meant for me."

Feather wiped away the banana cream and piecrust (for that is what it was) and tried to flip it to the floor with several ineffective waves of his wrist. A good deal of goo still stuck to his hands. His feathers were a mess. It was hard to get this stuff off. He scooped it out of his ears and wished he liked pie half as much as he liked doughnuts. Somehow the soft, wet texture of cream pie could never match the chewy heft of a fine, caky, frosted old-fashioned.

When he finally pried his eyes open, Feather saw Urania standing over him. She seemed to be looking at him and over her shoulder at the same time. The Human was gone.

"Quick!" said Urania. "We've got to get out of here!"

Feather staggered to his feet, and together the two Muses headed for the exit. They emerged into a vast outdoor parking lot. The sun was just setting. The sky was blazing pink. Here and there a windshield reflected the sun's rays like brilliant lighthouse beacons. Streams of Humanity emerged from the mall and divided into smaller rivulets that trickled into the ocean of cars. These streams were not flowing smoothly. People seemed to be tripping, slipping, and falling down. Cooked fruit and crust were everywhere, as if a bakery truck had crashed and flung its load all over the pavement.

A fresh blueberry pie hurtled overhead and exploded with a *pof* against the windshield of a Chevrolodge Exploiter SUV. The two Muses began dodging and cutting back as they crossed the lot. Feather stepped in a gluey yellow mass attached to a pie plate, but he hurried on as best he could, with a lopsided *galumph-clack galumph-clack galumph-clack.*

They zigzagged out of the lot and into the surrounding desert. Within minutes, they were in a cactus-covered landscape of saguaro and prickly pear. The mall disappeared from view behind a jumble of boulders. The Muses walked (actually, one of them went with a rolling limp) until they came to the base of a high, vertical cliff. All was quiet. Urania pressed an inconspicuous stone, no different, apparently, from any of the other scrabble of rocks that littered the foot of the escarpment.

A door opened in the rockface.

They hurried through, the door closed silently behind them, and they found themselves once more in the familiar, arid landscape of Kokonino County, land of the Muses. A rising moon lighted their way through dry gullies and over stony hills.

Soon they parted. Urania strode off toward her mountaintop observatory, while Feather clumped ahead toward his modest cottage. At last it came into sight, a snug little building shaped like an onion, nestled among neatly tended and productive gardens. He paused to admire the view. He waggled his foot. The pie refused to come off.

He heard a tiny squeal of laughter.

The Muse spun around. Behind him on the path was something dangerous. Something disturbing. Something that should not be.

He saw a small, familiar, moonlit face framed by a tangled, curly mat of dark hair. The face was laughing at him.

A Human had come to Kokonino County.

2

An Inhuman Story

As FEATHER STARED at the girl, her laughter subsided. Her face soon settled back into the alert, wary, but rather gloomy expression the Muse had seen at the mall.

"Don't you try to hurt me," she growled.

"Why on earth would I do something like that?" Feather asked. Humans said the strangest things. He wondered if he would ever understand them. Plants were so much easier.

"I'm not going back," said the girl.

"Yes, back. Good idea. You should definitely go back."

"Try and make me!"

Feather had no idea how to make anyone do anything. He had once vaguely heard something about carrots and sticks, and although the stick part was rather mysterious, he understood carrots pretty well.

"If I give you a carrot, will you promise to go back?" he asked at last. At the mention of food, the girl's eyes lit up eagerly. She did look hungry.

"Three carrots," she replied.

The two of them descended the gentle slope to Feather's abundant garden. He pulled a carrot from its bed and handed it to his companion, who made quick work of it, and also a second, and a third. Feather beckoned her to the cottage. Too many carrots, he thought, could turn your eyeballs orange. Better to vary her diet.

A few minutes later, after hosing the lemon meringue off his feet and his face, Feather laid out a vegetarian feast of bean soup, corn, and greens, which the girl devoured with gusto. Occasionally she glanced up to take in the snug little room. It was a plant lover's paradise. Hoes, rakes, shears, shovels, trowels, watering cans, and other gardening tools hung in perfect order on one wall, while another wall supported a tall cabinet packed with oversized jars and crocks full of grains, dried peas, and lentils. Their rainbow of muted green, orange, yellow, and golden brown glowed in the warm light of a fragrant wood fire. On the floor, neat rows of bins bulged with winter vegetables: golden squashes, deep red beets, and a motley assortment of carrots, turnips, parsnips, and potatoes. Overhead hung a wire basket of onions and a number of potted plants, all expertly pruned.

A bowl of tired-looking, wrinkly fruit rested on the

table. Feather always kept fruit on hand. He knew he should eat it, but somehow the time never seemed right, and it tended to sit long and get old. . . .

After a lengthy silence, Feather cleared his throat. "O.K., time to go back, um—what's your name?" he said.

"Name's Emma. And I'm not going back!"

Feather was startled. "Emma, you promised! Didn't you?"

Emma shrugged and stirred her spoon through the leftovers. "I lied."

"B-but . . . you *have* to go back! What about school? Don't you miss your parents?"

She glared at him. "Of course I miss my parents! But I can't go back to them!"

"Oh, come on! Why not? I'm sure they'll be thrilled to see you."

"Because," muttered Emma bitterly, "I don't have any parents."

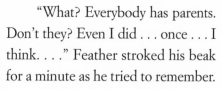

"What? Everybody has parents. Don't they? Even I did . . . once . . . I think. . . ." Feather stroked his beak for a minute as he tried to remember.

"My parents," said Emma quietly, "were killed in a car crash when I was four years old."

Feather looked at his feet. He felt he may have put one of them in his mouth, but no, there they both were, still flat on the floor.

"Where do you live now? Is there a nice garden?" he asked.

Emma looked at him strangely and went on. "After the accident, I stayed in foster homes for three years. Nobody kept me for long. I was too wild, they said. Destructive, they called me. And mean. This was so totally unfair! I never hurt anyone! At least, not badly. And I never broke anything. On purpose. And it wasn't expensive. Or not very. Anyway, no one would have me for long. Nobody, that is, until the Drinkwaters."

"The Drinkwaters?"

"Yes. Very nice people. I went to their house when I was seven. They were so sweet. So patient. They never, ever raised their voices at me. And I pulled some pretty good ones on them, too, especially Mr. Drinkwater . . . Darien Drinkwater . . . he's so funny-looking. . . ." She suddenly chuckled, then just as suddenly grew serious again. "But he never did anything but sigh, and then he'd fix what I'd broken, or go to the doctor, or whatever."

"To the doctor?"

"To get his butt bandaged."

"Bandaged?"

"On account of the burns, you know?"

"The b—"

"Never mind! The point is, he always put up with me."

"And what about her?" asked Feather.

Emma sighed. "Mrs. Drinkwater died last year."

Feather wondered what kind of flowers they had at her funeral, but he kept his thoughts to himself.

"After she died," continued Emma, "Mr. Drinkwater seemed to . . . change."

"Change how?"

"More irritable . . . less patient . . ."

"Yam?" Feather offered a yellow hunk.

The girl shot him a look. "No, thank you," she said tartly as Feather reflected painfully on the limitations of vegetables as a solution to Humanity's problems.

"Anyway, a couple of weeks ago, when I came home from school, Mr. Drinkwater was sitting in the hall, just inside the front door. This was pretty unusual. He didn't seem like himself at all. It's hard to describe. He's a really big guy, but he always used to hold himself up very straight." She stood and held her head high to illustrate. "Now he was all . . . in a heap." She slumped back into her chair. "He looked like mashed potatoes with arms."

"Potatoes are *loaded* with vitamin C," said Feather helplessly.

She went on. "He was doing something strange. Beside him, on a little round table, was a collection of glass figurines that his wife had collected. Miniature horses, swans with delicate necks, and a chubby penguin, all in glass. Now Drinkwater had set them out in rows and was moving them around, some going this way, some going that way, and he kept changing the arrangement, as if he couldn't quite get it right.

"Then he said something that sent shivers down my spine. He said, 'Show me again how it happened, Emma. Remind me. The accident.'

"'How did it go?' he said. 'Your car was here—' and he set down one of the horses. Then I realized that he was making a little model of a street intersection. 'And over here, were there other cars?' He put some other horses and swans down in a row, crosswise to the first horse, like a stream of traffic coming from the horse's right. 'And over here, on the left,' laying down the glass penguin on its face, 'that's the brick truck? Does that look right, Emma?'

"My heart was racing. He was recreating the accident that killed my parents!"

Feather thought of a few herbs that could calm a racing heart.

"'And finally,' he said, 'here comes the other car.' He moved another horse up behind the first one. 'Does this look right?' he asked again. He bumped his horse's nose into the other one's tail, pushing it forward in front of the penguin. 'And then what happened?'

"'THIS!' I yelled. I know I shouldn't have done it, but I couldn't stop myself. I took hold of the fat little glass penguin, and I crashed it into all the other toys. First into the horse that was my car, then into the swans and the other

horses. Everything fell to the floor. It all broke into bits, of course. All Mrs. Drinkwater's precious things.

"In the old days, Mr. Drinkwater would have just sighed and smiled. Such a sweet smile he used to have. But not this time. He jumped out of his chair. He was shaking with rage. His face was . . . I don't know . . . all squinched up so I could barely see his eyes. He was totally shaking and squinch-faced.

"'I'VE HAD ENOUGH!' he yelled."

"Of what?" asked Feather.

"That's just what I said. And with a roar he answered, 'Of YOU, you weasel, of YOU! Enough of your tricks! Enough of your damage! I've had ENOUGH! Done ENOUGH! Put up with ENOUGH!' And he raised up his hand—"

"You might have offered him some chamomile tea," suggested Feather. "It can be very calming."

Emma rolled her eyes. "Are you kidding? I ducked under his arm and ran to my room as fast as I could. He ran after me. He was huffing and puffing like a bicycle pump on legs. But I was fast enough to slam the door ahead of him and lock it. You should have heard him pounding! I thought he would punch right through it . . . but after a while, he must have gotten control of himself. He quieted down. I heard him walking away. Eventually, I decided it was safe to come out.

"For a couple of days he was his old self. It was as if the weird thing had never happened. But this didn't last long. He started muttering under his breath. 'Enough, enough,' he would grunt like a pig. Whatever I did seemed to make him mad. I didn't know what to expect, and I didn't want to stick around and find out.

"So I ran away. I went to the mall . . . I saw you and your friends . . . you told me one of them could help . . . but then she ran away! I decided to follow you.

"I don't want to go back! I don't want to live with any more strangers! I don't want to live with people who think I'm trouble! But I don't want to live like a runaway, either! It's no fair! What did I ever do to deserve this?" She burst into tears.

"All I want," she went on when her sobs had subsided, "is a real home. I just want to live with sweet, reasonable people who understand me and love me the way I am. I want my family! Why can't I be with my own flesh and blood like everybody else?"

And she cocked an eye at Feather to see if he was paying attention.

3

Intelligent Air

"Don't worry!" said Feather brightly. "We're here to help!"

"*Who's* here to help?" asked Emma.

"We are," said Feather before he could stop himself. "The Muses."

"Excuse me?" said Emma. "*Muses?* Isn't a Muse something from a dead civilization?"

Feather looked down at himself. He did look a little historical.

"We're *New* Muses," he said, "and we're very much alive! We find people who need help, and we give them useful suggestions." He drew himself up proudly to his full height, which was just a shade under five feet. "I'm Feather, Muse of Plants."

"What are you talking about?"

"If you'll help me wash these dishes," he replied, "I'll explain."

Together they gathered up the bowls, pots, and plates that littered the table. Feather carefully spooned the leftovers into smaller bowls and put them in the fridge. This involved a good deal of rearrangement and bother, since the shelves were very crowded. Once everything was wedged back in, Feather ladled some hot water into a basin and began washing dishes. He handed each dripping plate to Emma, who dried and stacked. As they worked, Feather told this story:

Once upon a time (he began), there were nine Muses. All of them were Greek. And they were all female. They were like junior goddesses, and each one specialized in an Ancient Greek art: dance, theater, history, epic poetry, lyric poetry, astronomy . . . and . . . and . . . three other ones I can't remember.

("Pottery?" asked Emma. "I read somewhere that the Greeks were good at pottery." "I don't know," replied Feather. "They're good at spinach pie, too, but I don't think they had a Muse for it.")

Ancient Greek artists (he went on) were the same as artists of any time and place: nervous, sweaty, and depressed. They would stare anxiously at their blank computer screens and wonder why there were never enough ideas, or else too many bad ones. Making art was *very* stressful.

("Are you sure the Ancient Greeks had computers?" asked Emma. "You're right," said Feather. "I meant to say typewriters.")

Nowadays, artists without ideas will get up, pace around the room, chew off a few fingernails, read the newspaper, write some e-mail, surf the Web, go out for coffee, eat too many muffins, take a short nap, wake up groggy, and feel sorry for themselves.

("Is that what artists do?" said Emma. "I had no idea.")

The Greeks (continued Feather) had a better way. They "invoked their Muse." This meant they would call on the Muse of their particular art, whatever it happened to be. With any luck, the Muse would answer. As she sang, ideas flowed straight into the artist's mind.

("How did that work?" asked Emma. "I don't know," said Feather, "but it must have been pretty low-tech. Maybe the Old Muses went door to door.")

It's really not so different today. Humans still need help, and we New Muses give them ideas. We communicate our thoughts using a top-secret technology called Intelligent Air. Intelligent Air allows us to watch people, listen to them, and whisper right into their ears. And no one ever suspects a thing!

Aside from the technology, there is one big difference between us and the ancients. The Greeks understood that ideas came from outside themselves. They knew the Muses were *real*. But today's self-centered Humans think ideas come from an "inner voice" in their own minds. People don't believe in us anymore! Well, if that's what they want to think, fine! All the better!

("How does Intelligent Air work?" asked Emma. "I can't explain it very well," Feather replied. "I specialize in plants, and Intelligent Air isn't very . . . organic.")

Of course, times have changed since Ancient Greece (he continued), and so have the nine arts. The New Muses have much more responsibility than the old ones ever did. We talk to everyone, not just artists. Now we have a Muse of Plants (that's me), plus Muses of Animals, Hardware, Software, Getting Along with People, Poetry, Astronomy, Music, and Factoids, or miscellaneous stuff.

So you see, there's a lot of talent here to help Humans like you.

("What makes you think there are any other humans like me?" asked Emma. "People aren't all the same, you know, like so many carrots!" "Carrots can be very different," said Feather, frowning, "but they all have one thing in common: they don't interrupt.")

Our work began when Chad and Aeiou—they're the Muses of Hardware and Software—first invented Intelligent Air. They saw how the new medium could be used to help Humanity, and they called on experts from all over the world to join them. Unlike the Old Muses, though, we don't wait to be "invoked." There are so many people in the world now, and they complain so much! And some people have real problems and never say anything. So we quietly seek out people with serious problems, and quietly we suggest solutions. We never try to draw attention to ourselves. ("Well . . . almost never," he qualified.)

The two of them sat for some time in silence, which was broken occasionally by the crackling fire and the burbling of Feather's stomach. At last, Emma spoke.

"And what became of the Old Muses?" she asked in a rather doubtful tone.

"Eight of them live in a retirement home not far from here. The ninth, Urania, is one of us. She's the Muse of Astronomy."

"I don't get it. Are you human, or what? Face it: you don't look very . . . godlike."

"Well . . . some of us used to be Human, but I don't think you could say we are anymore. Some of us were never Human to begin with, like Crraw, the Muse of Bad Poetry. He's a crow and always has been. And Urania must be at least twenty-five hundred years old—that doesn't sound very Human. And of course we're not all female— I say, what's the matter?"

Emma was frowning deeply. She leaped up from the table, grabbed a turnip, and threw it at Feather as hard as she could. He dodged, and the vegetable flew past his head and crunched into the fireplace, sending up sparks and a hiss of steam. Feather seemed to be a target today. He sighed. What had he ever done to anyone?

"I don't believe you!" shouted the girl. "Two–thousand–year–old astronomers!" An apple sailed by. "Talking crows! Intelligent Air!" A rutabaga bounced off Feather's beak. "AS IF! I must admit, when I first met you, I wouldn't have given you much credit for imagination, but was I ever wrong! That's the most *unbelievable* story I've ever heard! If you 'Muses' are so busy *helping* people, then how come the world is such a *mess?*" She sat down and glared.

"Y-you don't understand," stammered Feather. "It's a big world . . . and there are only nine of us! We can't do everything! And besides, sometimes we . . . um . . . have our own problems. Some of the Muses aren't always so . . . nice . . . to each other . . . and sometimes we . . . we . . . er . . . get in each other's way. . . ."

"Stupid me," muttered Emma through clenched teeth. She strode to the door. "I thought I was following you into another world, a better world where I could be happy at last! Instead you turn out to be just another costumed freak with a story to tell. I'm so . . . disappointed!"

By now Feather was seriously alarmed. It was his mission to help people, and here, unquestionably, was someone who needed help. He had to do something. Impulsively, he reached into his pocket and pulled out an orange, plastic ball studded with small switches and dials. It was about the size and color of a lumpy tangerine. He ran his gloved fingers over the familiar form. He flicked and spun and adjusted.

Suddenly, in the air above the table, where a moment

before there had been only empty space, a picture appeared. Hanging in midair like a giant, disembodied, three-dimensional television screen—only clearer—was the image of a street.

Emma stopped in her tracks. "Awesome," she said. "That's my street. How did you do that?"

"Intelligent Air," said Feather.

He spun a dial, and the image flickered. Slowly it began to change, then faster and faster. Many houses flashed by, until Emma shouted, "Wait! That's my house!"

Now they were inside the house, looking at an entry hall. Feather looked at Emma. She was trembling. "That's Drinkwater's chair!" she exclaimed nervously. Splinters of glass still glittered through clots of dust; apparently no one had swept up in some time.

"May I see my room?" Emma whispered hoarsely.

She directed Feather, whose expert fingers wheeled the terminal's fine-tuning knobs, across the hall, up the stairs, and to the right, until they could see a door covered with drawings and paintings and notes. A hand-lettered sign in crayon read KEEP OUT. The door was ajar. Emma gave a little shriek. "It shouldn't be open," she quavered. They looked inside.

Inside the room was a man. To Feather, the plant expert, he looked like any other Human. Nothing special about him at all. Except he was rather large. Huge, in fact. And ghostly pale. His bare arms looked like two gigantic white loaves of uncooked bread dough hanging out of his greasy undershirt. But otherwise, he looked totally normal.

Actually, his head looked pretty doughy, too. In fact, thought Feather, the whole man appeared to be made out of several shapeless gobs of dough slapped together by an oversized baker. Puffy arms and legs tapered to small hands and feet, as if the man's maker had run out of raw material and suddenly twisted off the ends into ragged little points. Aside from that, he was ordinary looking, at least if you ignored his exceptionally tiny eyes and the tufts of hair that stuck out everywhere in random directions.

The small, delicate hands were busily rifling through a chest of drawers.

"Ugh," whispered Feather. "Who's *that?* He needs *baking!*"

"That's Darien Drinkwater," Emma whispered back. "He doesn't look very well. And he's going through my stuff!"

Drinkwater was making a strange noise in the back of his throat, halfway between a hum and a growl. It rose and fell regularly, as if he were singing a song to himself again and again. "Where is it?" he sang. "Where *is* it, where *is* it, where *is* it?" He closed the dresser drawers with surprising care and began opening

small boxes on top of the chest. At last, he seemed to find what he was looking for. He held up a small piece of paper triumphantly, his eyes gleaming like two shiny blueberries surrounded by folds of dough.

"Oh no!" gasped Emma.

"What's that?" asked Feather. He zoomed the Intelligent Air image in to read the paper. It seemed to be gibberish. "'QAZXRCGB,'" Feather read. "What's that supposed to mean?"

"I don't know," moaned Emma. "That piece of paper is one of the only things I have left in the world from my parents. Even though it's torn and it doesn't make sense, I've kept it. And now, that . . . that . . . *Drinkwater* is taking it!"

Feather tried to think of some way plants could help.

With trembling hands, Drinkwater produced a second piece of paper from his wallet and held it up next to the first one. His hum rose in pitch to something more like a whine.

"Ohmigosh!" exclaimed Emma. "I forgot all about the other half!"

The two scraps fitted together perfectly, and their messages, if that was what they were, meshed seamlessly. Still, the text made no sense. It read:

QAZXRCGB97YR00WWBB

Emma whispered urgently. "I just remembered!

When the Drinkwaters took me in, I had two things from my parents. One was a slip of paper. The other was a key. The key I gave to Mr. Drinkwater for safekeeping, and the paper I tore into two pieces. I kept half, and I gave the other to the Drinkwaters, to show I wanted them to be like my new real parents. I completely forgot about it until just now!"

"Shouldn't we be writing this down?" asked Feather sensibly.

"Where's a pencil?" asked Emma.

"I don't know!" said Feather.

"What am I supposed to use, then?" asked Emma.

"Dip a carrot in beet juice and write on the table," said Feather.

"Where are the carrots?" asked Emma.

"In the bin behind you!" said Feather.

"O.K., I have everything," said Emma. "Now, what does it say again?"

Feather looked at the image, but the paper was gone. Drinkwater had put it in his wallet. Emma pounded the table in frustration until all her spunkiness drained away. "Who can help me?" she whispered to no one in particular.

Feather considered what to do. If the Muse of Plants didn't know how to decipher a coded message or soften the heart of a large, doughy man, there were Muses who did. Mimi, Muse of Getting Along with People, was good with Humans. She could probably whisper something helpful to Drinkwater. Urania, Muse of Astronomy, had a talent for math. She could work on the code if they ever had another chance to copy it. Even Chad, Muse of Hardware, might possibly help with . . . with . . . with—suddenly, Feather remembered what Chad could help with.

"Come on, Emma! Let's go and see Chad!"

4

Chad's Lab

CHAD, FEATHER REMEMBERED, could help him with doughnuts. It had occurred to Feather at some point during his day at the mall that he could avoid the Krusty-Glop shop completely if he had his very own doughnut-making machine. Chad, he was sure, could build such a thing. Chad, the Muse of Hardware, could build anything. There might even be some way he could help Emma, too.

Feather opened the door, and they emerged into the chilly, desert night. Beyond the green oasis, sand stretched away in all directions. Great rocky hills jutted upward in the distance, dimly illuminated by the countless twinkling stars scattered across the black sky like pale candy sprinkles on a chocolate-frosted, double-glazed— No, thought Feather. Banish that thought!

They followed the path to Chad's laboratory, which lay just over the first hill and past the second cactus on the right. Soon they could make out the blocky silhouette of the main building below a row of tall chimneys that spewed a sort of mist into the sky. To the left rose a dark dome, which housed a telescope that Chad had once built for Urania as a favor, and which now served as the laboratory's main entrance. Feather led Emma toward the round shadow. Nearer the building, the night seemed very dark. He stepped on something sharp. It must have been one of the thousands of stray nuts and bolts that littered every surface in and around the lab. With throbbing foot, Feather crept forward. His shin smacked a table-sized spool of copper bridge cable. He winced and saw stars—and not familiar stars either, but strange ones in strange colors he had seen only once before, after drinking an especially potent mixture of cactus-and-mushroom tea. He reminded himself to ask Urania about mental astronomy sometime.

"Are you O.K.?" Emma whispered.

"Yes," moaned Feather. "And you?"

"No problem." And in fact, Emma did seem more adept than Feather at stepping around the sharp bits.

They reached the dome and peered inside. It was deserted. A faint humming noise came from the motorized mounts that turned the telescope toward its target in the slowly rotating sky. Through a slit in the dome's roof they could see stars again—real ones this time—and the black form of the telescope itself.

"Can we look?" asked Emma.

"I suppose," said Feather indifferently.

The girl hurried up a short flight of stairs to the telescope's base. She oohed with pleasure and beckoned Feather to join her. He groped his way forward, mounted the steps, and peered into the eyepiece.

He shrieked.

There, magnified to immense size against the blackness of space, was something round, something golden, something with a hole so big it surrounded an entire planet. Feather beat his head against the telescope. He moaned and looked again, and again he saw it: the rings of Saturn, a great, glowing cosmic doughnut, nearly a billion miles away and forever out of reach. He fainted.

WHEN FEATHER CAME TO, Emma was fanning his face with a scrap of sheet metal. The breeze was refreshing. He wished it would never end. But with her other hand, Emma was pointing at a sliver of light on the opposite wall, where a door stood slightly ajar.

"Listen," she whispered. "I hear voices."

Feather stood up, brushed off a few stray bolts, and crept to the door. He heard:

"Missed, missed, missed! Worthless piece of junk!"
said one voice.

"Not worthless," said a second voice. "The problem
is only that the machine lacks precision. It needs to be
more precise."

"It needs to be more *precise*," sneered the first voice.
"Chad, when people said you were a genius, I believed
them. But now I see they were wrong, wrong, wrong! Any
idiot can see it needs to be more precise!"

Feather knew the voices all too well. One, of course,
was Chad's. The other, unfortunately, belonged to Kokopelli, Muse of Tunes, who was also Muse of Tricks and all
kinds of malicious mischief. Taking Emma's hand, Feather
crept toward the slightly open door and peeked through.

 He could see Kokopelli's angular
silhouette hopping around the lab
like a dancing shadow, flute in hand,
spiky hair waving. This could be
awkward. It was hard to get Kokopelli to take any problem seriously,
and Feather and Emma had two of
them. Feather beckoned the Human to wait and listen.

Chad's voice replied, "We came close." Everything
about Chad was calm. He never seemed to panic; in his
view, science and engineering always go one step at a time,
by small adjustments, with patience. Noise, worry, and
alarm only slow things down.

"Not close enough!" whined Kokopelli. "If all I
wanted to do is throw pies at Feather, we'd be done! I can

do it by hand! He's so dumb, he doesn't see it coming from two feet away! Heeheehee!" Feather blushed. It was true, more or less. "But Urania's harder," Kokopelli went on. "She's smarter. And even worse: she's on to me. I can't get within arm range! I just can't connect with that moony face! I need this machine to work! AARGH!" Kokopelli was practically sobbing now. His normally spiky hair sagged like strands of black spaghetti wilting in boiling water.

"Why Urania?" asked Chad.

"That is none of your business. Just tell me, is there hope?"

"Adjustments are still possible," said Chad quietly.

"Adjustments?" Kokopelli suddenly perked up.

Feather widened the crack of the open door enough to see in. The usual heaps of spare parts littered the laboratory floor. The room's walls supported—barely— sagging shelves full of spectrometers, micrometers, manometers, and other meters; nuts, bolts, screws, rivets, and nails; wrenches, saws, hammers, screwdrivers, and drills; test tubes, vacuum tubes, cathode-ray tubes, and inner tubes; transistors, resistors, thermistors, capacitors; spools of wire, connectors, plugs, cables, and chunks of dismantled computers. Someone once said that Chad's lab had everything but the kitchen sink, but this was false. Feather saw several of them jumbled in the corner like a giant's alphabet blocks.

In the midst of the mess was a monstrous contraption. A bulky, squat mountain of machinery loomed above Chad and Kokopelli. Gears, pulleys, belts, wires, and glowing computer screens combined to form a mass of cubes and cylinders, above which towered a tall arm, slightly off the vertical like a tilted flagpole. An oversized mitt at the tip held a large, dripping strawberry cream pie.

"Let's review how this machinery works," Chad continued. "You recently gave Urania a new hair ribbon, which was secretly implanted with a powerful radio transmitter. The ribbon sends a signal to Global Positioning System (GPS) satellites in outer space. The GPS computes her exact latitude and longitude and beams the data to computers here in my lab, which adjust the flinger arm," he gestured upward, "to catapult a pie in her direction. Remember?"

"NO, I DON'T REMEMBER!"

"Our problem," Chad continued, "is that GPS isn't accurate enough. It can only pinpoint Urania's position to within ten feet. Imagine a ten-foot circle on the ground; we know she's in there somewhere, but not exactly where."

Kokopelli started loudly playing his flute.

"The second problem," continued Chad, shouting over the music, "is that Urania is a moving target. It takes time for the pie to travel from here to there. By the time it lands, Urania may not be where we expected. The computer can calculate her speed at launch time and predict where she's going, but what if she stops? What if she turns and changes direction? You see the problem?"

The flute music had died. The little imp made no response. His head was drooping. Feather could hear gentle snoring, like the purring of a cat—one of the smaller, more dangerous wildcats, he thought, an ocelot or a lynx. Chad coughed.

"I'm awake!" shrieked Kokopelli with a start.

"Did you follow what I was saying?"

"Not exactly. Can you put it in words I can understand?"

"With this setup," Chad waved sadly at the heap of gear, "we'd be lucky to hit the broadside of a barn."

"So the flinger's a flop?"

"Unless . . ."

"Please. Just give a hint. Spare me the details."

"Unless we use Smart Pies."

"Smart Pies? Don't all pies smart when they hit you?" The Muse of Tricks cackled at his own joke. So, to Feather's surprise, did Emma.

"If there were some way we could put intelligence directly into the pies themselves . . ." Chad hummed vaguely. "For instance, suppose we could capture images, pictures of the targets, and wire them right into the pie's memory circuits . . ."

"You're loooozing me," sang Kokopelli.

"Then, once they get near the targets, if the pies could steer themselves . . . hmmm . . . hmmm . . .

"I have it!" exulted Chad, flailing his arms and knocking over an old computer monitor, which exploded on the floor. "Listen—this is brilliant. We'll—"

"I said, spare me the details!" screamed Kokopelli.

"Let me put it this way, Koko. Do you know anyone who owes you a favor?"

"Could be arranged," said the imp.

"Someone who'd stay near the, er, objective at all times?"

"Someone kind of stupid, who'd just sit there and not think too much, you mean?"

"Can we say patient, not stupid, if you don't mind?"

"Whatever. Sure. Why not?"

"Well, then," said Chad, "we could . . . ," and his voice dropped to an inaudible whisper for several minutes. The words *camera* and *broadcast* and *relay* and *image* reached their ears, but the sense of it escaped Feather completely.

"Wow," whispered Emma.

"Brilliant!" crowed Kokopelli. "Chad, I take back everything bad I ever said about you! And everything anyone else ever said, too! How soon can this gizmo be ready?"

"Tomorrow morning, if I put in an all-nighter."

"Rah!" cheered Kokopelli, dancing around the room as if he had tarantulas in his underwear.

An all-nighter, thought Feather sadly. Chad would be busy until the following day. No time tonight to think about a doughnut-making machine. Or Emma's problem, either. He sighed deeply. His stomach voiced a complaint that sounded like a police siren played backward in slow motion.

At the sound, all conversation stopped. "Who's there?" said Chad and Kokopelli together.

Feather opened his mouth to speak and froze in that position. The Human, he thought. Had he been out of his mind to bring her along? Everyone knew Kokonino County was a Human-Free Zone, and he had knowingly welcomed one in. Fed her. Told her Muse secrets. Even showed her Intelligent Air. What would happen if the others found out? He promised himself he would think things through more carefully next time. Probably.

"Oh, Feather, it's only you," said Chad, coming to the door. "Come in."

"Shouldn't you close your mouth?" said Kokopelli. "A piece of meat might fly in."

Feather looked around. Emma was gone.

"I . . . ah . . . you . . . he . . . we . . . wah . . . um . . . ," said Feather.

"Oh, Feather, you're so perfect!" Kokopelli smiled— or at least he seemed to be smiling. His shadowy face concealed his features completely. "Why don't you go home and get some sleep? It's the middle of the night, and I need to see you in the morning. I want you fresh! Rested! Alert!"

"See me? In the morning?" Feather's thoughts came at the speed of plant growth. After a time, he decided that Emma, wherever she was, would be safe. Kokonino County harbored no dangerous life forms, aside from Kokopelli. And he was here.

"Yes . . . right. It's late. I'll be going now. See you in the morning." Why was that, again? "Good night."

On the way home, he stubbed his toe on a kitchen sink, barked his shin on a refrigerator compressor, and fell over backward into a cactus.

5
A Plot Is Hatched

RAP RAP RAP RAP RAP! The sound hammered into Feather's brain like a railroad spike. He slowly opened his eyes. His head, shins, and toes throbbed, and his mouth tasted like stale broccoli. He wondered if his tongue were really necessary. Where had he been last night? Suddenly he remembered the Human, and his heart began to throb in time with everything else. He had to find her! Make her leave Kokonino County! Before the others found out! The pounding continued. Feather rose stiffly from bed, pushed his sore toes into his orange slippers, shuffled to the door, and opened it.

There stood Kokopelli, Muse of Tricks and Tunes. Beside him stood Emma. Both of them were laughing.

The angular little sprite, carrying a package under each arm, had been dancing impatiently on the threshold.

Beside him, Emma looked rumpled and sleepy but happy, like someone who had just stayed out all night for the first time. When the door opened, Kokopelli barged past Feather, laid his boxes on the table, and sat down. Emma followed him.

"My main Muse!" the imp shouted cheerfully. "What took you so long? Do you have any coffee brewed?"

"No . . . sorry . . . no coffee." Coffee had always seemed a little too . . . meaty to Feather, and besides, it speeded him up. He preferred to remain slow.

"Never mind! I've had fourteen cups already!" Kokopelli squirmed in his seat. "But, Feather," he went on, "why didn't you introduce me to your little Human friend earlier? She's really remarkable! We've been having the most marvelous time!"

Feather gaped and scratched his beak. "Y-you have?"

"Yes," put in Emma. "Koko has already been a big help! He got me the coded message from Drinkwater!"

"Kokopelli . . . helped?" Feather looked at Kokopelli, who seemed to be studying the back of his hand.

"He's so clever," Emma continued. "When he heard my story, he knew what to do right away."

"He did?"

"Of course, you lummox! Easiest thing in the world—for me!" said Kokopelli. "Dialed in the IA network and peeked at her house. Inspired a couple of neighbor boys to sneak out of their bedrooms for some midnight skateboarding. It didn't take much to convince them to put a rock through Drinkwater's window!"

Emma picked up the story excitedly. "When the crash woke up Drinkwater, Kokopelli whispered in his ear that thieves were trying to steal his papers. You should have seen him! I never knew how fast the big guy could fly! He looked like a hippo on stilts! He scampered to his study and opened up the metal strongbox where he keeps all his valuables. The first thing he checked was the piece of paper from my parents!"

"Quick as a wink, I put it in ink," said Kokopelli. "*Some* of us always have a pen when we need it." Kokopelli waved his empty hand, and suddenly a pen and a piece of paper appeared. How did he *do* that? He showed the paper to Feather. Written in quick, nervous strokes, it read:

QFNBSDBL87YR00WWCB

Kokopelli handed the scrap to the grateful girl, who looked at it with a tremulous mixture of sadness, hope, and excitement.

"Now I can take it to Urania and get it deciphered," she said. "She's good at math and secret codes, isn't that right?"

Kokopelli coughed. "That reminds me, Feather! Look here! I've brought you a present! Pick a package!" He pointed at the two boxes he had set on the table. Both of them were long, narrow packages tightly wrapped in gift paper, identical in shape and size, except that one was green and one was red.

Feather looked at them sleepily. He saw no difference. He waved at the green one randomly.

"Good!" cried Kokopelli. "You can have that one right now! The other one is for afterward!"

"Afterward?"

"After you do me a little favor. Would you like to see what's in it?" Without waiting for an answer, Koko ripped off the red wrapper with a swift jerk to reveal a doughnut carton emblazoned with the Krusty-Glop logo. Feather took a deep breath. He felt faint. Kokopelli slowly opened the lid. Inside was an astonishing assortment: Kranberry

Krullers, Lemon Yellow Fever, Chocolate Fudge Belly Bomb, Louder Powder, Amazing Glaze, Banana Piranha, and more of Feather's favorites. A sugary scent ascended his nostrils.

Feather had already forgotten whether this was the Now Box or the Afterward Box, but his fingers voted for Now. He lunged for the nearest doughnut, a glistening gray-blue, fish-shaped confection called Trout No Doubt, but before his hand could touch sugar, Kokopelli snatched the package away.

"Ah-ah-ah!" he admonished. "This one's for later! You have to do me a favor first, remember?"

Feather noticed with alarm that the doughnuts seemed to have disappeared completely. How did Kokopelli *do* that? At least the other box was still available. Feather grasped it firmly in his orange paws. Kokopelli made no move to stop him.

Feather glanced at Emma. She seemed to be following the conversation avidly.

"This favor," said Feather. "Is it something difficult?"

"No."

"Unpleasant?"

"Not for you."

"Illegal?"

"Probably not."

"Will I hate myself in the morning?"

"Will you miss a dozen assorted Krusty-Glop doughnuts?"

"What do I have to do?"

"Spend some time with Urania," said the Muse of Tricks. "Lots of time. All the time, actually. Stay as close as you can. Keep an eye on her. Stare like a puppy in love. Whatever you do, DON'T TAKE YOUR EYES OFF HER."

This sounded easy enough. Not especially polite, but easy.

"And what is she supposed to think about this?"

"That you want to spend time with your friend."

Feather pondered. "And how do I know you'll give me . . . um . . . that package when I'm done?"

Kokopelli gave a little bark of laughter. "Feather, don't disappoint me! I've always thought of you as a trusting Muse, not a shrewd one. Don't ever change! Look, I've already given you one present, which you can keep with absolutely no obligation. If you don't want the second box of doughnuts, fine. Don't help me. Enjoy the first one, and I'll be running along."

Feather looked at the box in his hands. Kokopelli had said, "Second box of doughnuts," so didn't that imply that the first box was also . . . ? And wouldn't that mean— he did the arithmetic on his fingers—two dozen in the end . . . ? He tightened his grip on the package.

"I'll do it," he said.

"Excellent. Now take off your headdress and shirt and give them to me."

Feather squawked briefly, but having promised, he obeyed the request. First, off came the feathered hood and overcoat, and then his green, sleeveless undershirt wriggled over his great beak and slipped into Kokopelli's outstretched hands. Emma giggled. As if from nowhere, the imp produced a narrow, black, plastic tube with a glistening lens at one end, a few batteries, a square chip of plastic, some wires, and a needle and thread. He began sewing the electronic items into the clothes.

"This digital camera," he muttered as the tube disappeared into the top of the headdress, with only its tiny lens peeking out at the front, "sees what you see. It runs off these batteries," he tucked them into the back of the hood, "and is turned on by this button." By this he meant the plastic square, which he deftly stitched into the front of Feather's shirt. Tangles of wires protruded from the neck holes of the garments. "When you get the signal, press the button once to turn on the camera. It takes pictures automatically every few seconds; you don't have to do a thing but point your face."

"What's the signal to turn it on?"

"Oh, you'll know it when it comes," said Koko with an unhelpful chuckle. "Now put your clothes back on."

The headdress felt lumpier and heavier than usual, but Kokopelli, after reaching under Feather's chin to connect all the wires, looked him over and declared him a sleek and stylish Muse. Emma agreed with a smile.

"You want me to take pictures of Urania?"

"Oh, Feather, it's good to have a friend as dumb as you!" cackled Kokopelli.

"And why did you say I'll be doing this?"

"I didn't!" Kokopelli began pumping Feather's hand vigorously. "But let me tell you, old friend, how grateful I am! You won't regret this little favor, Feather, my Muse! I know I won't! Well, much as I'd like to stay and talk, now I must go! There are pies to be loaded! Circuits to set! You go, too! Go to Urania! But have some breakfast first. It may be a long day. Good-bye!"

Feather felt certain that he should ask some important questions, but Kokopelli was gone. Exactly where he went was not entirely clear, but he was definitely gone, or fairly definitely. You never knew with Kokopelli.

Somewhere in the world, it was feeding time at the

zoo. A zookeeper was rolling a wheelbarrow loaded with thick cuts of red meat into the lion house. The roars echoing off the walls very closely resembled the sound just now being made by the Muse of Plant's ample stomach. It was feeding time at Feather's. He eagerly tore the green wrapper off the Now Box and looked for the Krusty-Glop logo. There was no Krusty-Glop logo. The box was plain, like a shoebox. The Muse flipped open the lid.

It was full of broccoli.

Kokopelli! How did he *do* that?

6

Urania

AFTER AN UNSATISFYING broccoli breakfast, Feather took Emma to see Urania, Muse of Astronomy. Emma, of course, hoped that Urania would help decipher her coded message, while Feather had a mission of his own. "Don't take your eyes off her," Kokopelli had said. The rig sewn into his hood chafed his scalp. His shirt felt bunchy and tight from the wires. He was so distracted and itchy, he failed to notice that Emma was carrying a black leather valise the size of a violin case with a monogrammed *C* in gold near its handle.

The desert morning was clear, bright, and silent, except for the crunching of their feet on the gravelly path. They climbed up gentle slopes and down shadowy ravines, passed through stands of snakelike ocotillo and stately saguaro saluting like soldiers, and avoided the cholla or "jumping cactus" that attaches itself to any unwary legs that brush it in passing. Occasionally a sunbathing lizard darted away on their approach, and vultures circled lazily in the sky. After an hour's walk, during which the temperature rose with the sun, the pair reached a sheer cliff. At its base stood a mailbox painted to look like the night sky, black with a smattering of white stars and moons, and lettered in red with the word *Urania*.

Cut into the rock before them, a steep staircase wound up the cliff to Urania's aerie. To Feather, who felt exercise was like broccoli—a little was enough—it looked endless. No wonder Urania was in such good shape. She had to take this path at least once a day just to fetch her mail. Carrying up groceries was more than Feather wanted to imagine. It seemed selfish of her to force visitors to hike just because she wanted to live near the stars. Who needs stars? he wondered, then grumpily remembered that astronomers made calendars, and calendars tell farmers when to plant. Frowning, he began to climb.

Up they went. Emma would scamper ahead until she found a cool resting spot, where she would sit and wait for the hefty, chuffing Muse of Plants to catch up. After an hour and a gallon of sweat, they reached the top of the mesa.

Several mysterious structures of an astronomical nature rose from the summit. The Muse of Astronomy, her cloak covering her head for shade, was bent over a table at the base of a stone stairway. She was drawing lines and circles

on large sheets of paper, while overhead an Intelligent Air image showed a group of high-school students having a lively discussion about sunspots. Whenever the students seemed stuck or confused, Urania would whisper a helpful suggestion. This is how the New Muses work.

"Urania," called Feather.

Urania jumped. She wheeled, her wrap swirling around her. It seemed to take her some time to lose her previous train of thought and return to Earth. When at last she realized what she was seeing, she clicked off Intelligent Air, drew herself up to her full height, and scowled imperiously.

"Is that a HUMAN?" she intoned in an operatic voice.

"Yes, but—"

Urania began stuffing papers into her robe. When her robe was full, she gathered them into her arms. When her arms were full, she dived behind the staircase and disappeared from view, showing only a golden-haired topknot peeking above the railing. This was a problem. Feather was supposed to keep his eyes on her.

"GET IT OUT OF HERE!" she screamed.

"No, wait, Urania! Please!" he moaned. "I'm supposed to—I mean, I *want* to see you."

"YOU KNOW THE RULES, FEATHER!"

Feather began a conversation with himself about thinking things through ahead of time. Just last night he had promised, and already . . . He called himself *Aphis glycines* and *Amanita muscaria* and Common Bladderwort and many other pests and poisons not worth mentioning. He felt a hand on his arm. It was Emma. She waved him back and signaled that she would like to approach Urania directly. Feather shrugged and motioned her on.

Carrying her leather case, the girl advanced toward the stone stairway. She stopped at the near side, keeping the structure between herself and Urania.

"IS SHE STILL THERE?" cried the Muse of Astronomy's fruity contralto.

"Excuse me, Ms. Urania, Your Stellarness," said Emma softly. "I know I'm not supposed to be here, but I've brought you something very important from Chad."

"You HAVE?"

She had? thought Feather.

There was a silence.

"What is it?"

Emma reached around the base of the stairs and pushed the black leather case toward the other side. Urania's hand reached out and pulled it toward her. Feather heard a zip and a rustle of papers. After a moment or two, Urania stood up, smiled, and approached them. With the bag under one arm, she threw her other arm around Emma's shoulders. Feather peered at her intently according to Kokopelli's instructions.

"Feather," she said warmly, "why didn't you tell me you'd brought such a *clever* one?"

Soon they were sipping iced tea, and Emma began describing her problem. Feather gazed in silence.

"Tell me about the auto accident," Urania said abruptly.

"A glass penguin ran into her parents' little horse," explained Feather helpfully.

They both gave him a look. He stared back at Urania.

"It happened like this," said Emma. "Our car was stopped at a red light. I was sitting in back, and my parents were in front. Suddenly we were rammed from behind. It happened so fast, I hardly knew what was going on. A car had rear-ended us. It must have been speeding. The driver probably never saw the red light. Our car shot into the traffic. . . ."

Urania had taken out a notebook and was sketching busily. She drew a diagram of the accident and showed it to Emma. "Something like this?" she asked. Emma confirmed that the sketch was accurate. "Yes," murmured Urania, "the other vehicle's momentum was transferred to your own. . . ."

"There was nothing anyone could do," said Emma. "A huge truck full of bricks was just barreling into the intersection from our left. It wiped out the front end of our car. Both my parents were killed. Sitting in back, I survived."

"You're very lucky," said Urania gravely.

"Yes, I suppose," sighed Emma. "All I have left from my parents is a coded message. I was hoping you could help me figure out what it means."

At the words *coded message,* Urania smiled eagerly. "Excellent!" she exclaimed. Coding and decoding were among her mathematical specialties. "May I see it?"

Emma handed her a piece of paper. Urania turned it over in her hands, rotated it this way and that, held it up to the light. She took pencil in hand and began jotting calculations on a large pad. "QFNBSDBL87YR00WWCB," she said slowly, "QFNBSDBL87YR00WWCB . . . Hmm . . . Did you write this down yourself, Emma?"

"No, Kokopelli copied it for me." Emma described how the Muse of Tricks had managed to look at the paper.

"Just as I thought," Urania muttered. "It looks like his handwriting. I'm sorry, Emma, but this is completely worthless."

"What?" Feather stole a sideways glance at Emma. She looked stunned.

"It's just the way the little guy is," said the astronomer. "Not very dependable, I'm afraid. Maybe he changed some letters on purpose, or made a copying mistake. Either way, the arithmetic doesn't add up."

Emma made a sound halfway between a sob and a growl.

"Don't give up, little moon child," said Urania soothingly. "Kokonino County is full of Muses who can help. You've only just begun." She turned to Feather, who had been dutifully staring at her the whole time. "Where should we go next, Feather? I think Mimi would be best. Perhaps she can persuade Mr. Drinkwater to show us the original again. Feather," she added, "why are you staring at me like that?"

"Um . . . um . . . like what?"

"Like a dog watching its owner peel carrots," she said. "You're making me nervous."

"Am I?" said Feather blandly, maintaining his unblinking gaze. "I'm sorry. I'm . . . I'm . . . only trying to show you how much I agree with you. Yes, we should absolutely see Mimi at once! I'll follow you wherever you want to go! Never leave your side for a minute!" At this, Urania twitched.

"You think Mimi can talk sense into Mr. Drinkwater?" asked Emma hopefully.

"If anyone can, she's the one," said Feather and Urania at the same time.

The three set off at once. Feather had to watch the path during the steep descent to avoid plunging a thousand feet to a hideous death on the jagged rocks and thorny cacti below, but once they reached the bottom, he resumed staring at Urania. And so the trio made their way across the desert, two facing steadily forward and one looking sideways and consequently stubbing his toes and bumping into things all along the path.

7

A Buried Safe

IT WAS WELL PAST NOON when they reached Mimi's cottage. Feather, absent-mindedly taking his eyes off Urania, noted with disapproval that the shrubbery needed trimming. Shutters hung from the windows at random angles. The house was always chaotic. In this way, Mimi showed the other Muses that her place was no better than anyone else's. A mess was her way of being nice.

Feather tapped on the door. Nothing happened. He knocked harder. At last he heard a slow, aimless shuffling sound, followed by rattling and scraping, then more shuffling. The door slowly opened. Apparently, Mimi was in the middle of a late breakfast. Her costume was wrinkled, and crumbs dotted her angular face. Feather immediately recognized them as the remains of a cheap, frozen fruit pie, thawed in the toaster for a quick meal. He sneered at the scent of synthetic strawberry. In the world of pastry, this was low stuff; you could burn your tongue on the shell while the filling was still cold.

"G'm'ng," mumbled Mimi, her eyes only half open.

"Good morning," said the three visitors in unison. The Muse of Getting Along with People regarded them sleepily for a few minutes. At last it dawned on her who her visitors were, and her face became a mask of fear. Emma she barely seemed to notice; it was clearly Urania who terrified her. Mimi looked wildly into the sky and backed into the house while grabbing blindly behind herself for the doorknob.

"Mimi," said Urania reproachfully, "you're not worried about the flying pies, are you?"

"Who—me?—worried! Ha-ha." Mimi laughed.

"Because the probability of your being hit by a pie aimed at me is really very low. Or I should say, was very low. It's about to get even lower." Urania patted the leather carrying case she still had slung under her arm.

Mimi looked dubious. "But I saw Feather get hit with a pie at the mall yesterday."

"Yes, you did." Urania shrugged.

"I suppose that means today his chances of being hit are lower than mine." Mimi glared at the Muse of Vegetables.

"Actually, it doesn't, but that's beside the point."

"The point? The point? What's *your* point, Urania?" The Muse of Getting Along could be surprisingly rude.

"The point," interrupted Emma, "is that I need your help."

"You do?" said Mimi. "You're a Human, aren't you? Please come in!" The Muse of Getting Along with People was one of the few Muses who felt comfortable with Humans. She had opposed making Kokonino County a Human-Free Zone from the beginning. Maybe this old disagreement explained why, despite her unfailing politeness to Humans, she could behave so badly to her fellow Muses. Glaring at Urania over Emma's head, Mimi ushered the three of them into her living room, where they told her the details of Emma's strange and awful story.

IT TOOK MIMI some time to find an Intelligent Air terminal. She looked on the kitchen table, where a heap of clothes snaked among the crumbs and puddles left over from many breakfasts; on the floor, where more clothes tangled with a spray of music CDs scattered randomly out of their jewel boxes; on the CD rack, where clothes half buried a collection of disks standing all aslant and an ancient scoop of ice

cream had strangely congealed. At last, she circled back to the kitchen table and found the device inside a half-empty bag of pretzels. Her terminal was black, to match her stereo.

She brushed off the salt and twirled the dial.

The hulking form of Mr. Drinkwater filled the air. He was sitting in his study, lost in thought. His tiny eyes were rolled back under the puffy folds of his eyelids, and his small right hand rubbed the lumps and stubble on his doughy cheek, while he muttered to himself in his strange singsong wheeze.

"What does it mean? What does it mean? What does it mean?" he said. "QAZ, QAZX, QAZXR . . . What language is that? Swahili? Finnish? Urdu? AAARGH!" He bellowed and brought down his fist on the table with a crash that lifted the Muses out of their chairs.

"This doesn't look too promising," said Mimi.

"What's that?" said Drinkwater, and he looked over his shoulder suspiciously. "Somebody there?"

"Sorry," mouthed Mimi silently to the others. She zoomed in to whisper in Drinkwater's ear.

"Maybe Emma can help you," she suggested sweetly and pulled back to see his reaction.

The doughy face purpled. His brows pulled down until his eyes disappeared into two deep shadows. "Yes . . . probably could . . . ," he said to himself.

Mimi nodded to the others and gave a thumbs-up.

"But no . . . no . . . NO!" Drinkwater went on. "I want no more to do with that . . . little . . . wrecking machine. . . ."

Mimi's face fell. She zoomed in again, until his ear filled the image. It wasn't pretty. "Emma has good qualities, too," she said. "She's bright, and imaginative, and has a great sense of fun."

"Rrrrh," growled the man. "I'll bet she thought it was fun when she set fire to my posterior!"

"Um . . . what?" said Mimi.

"No, no," he said, "I've already given her everything I ever owed her and more. I'm done with the girl. DONE DONE DONE!" Again he was yelling and pounding the table.

"But—"

"I'LL FIGURE THIS OUT FOR MYSELF!"

"Couldn't you just ask him to take a look at the paper?" asked Emma.

"WHO SAID THAT?" roared Darien Drinkwater. He leaped from his chair and looked around wildly. "There's nobody here . . . but I swear I hear voices. . . ."

With that, Mimi clicked off the image. "He's hopeless," she said. "What a temper! Is there anyone else we can try?"

"There's my teacher, Mrs. Krishnamurti," said Emma doubtfully. "She's sent me to the principal's office like a thousand times, but I don't think she hates me. She might listen to you."

The Intelligent Air image flickered, bent, dissolved, and reformed. Now they were looking over a teacher's shoulder at a classroom. One desk was empty. The viewpoint spun around, and they could see the teacher, a slender woman with dark skin, black hair drawn back in a very long braid, and numerous slender golden bracelets that surrounded her slender wrists. Behind her the chalkboard was covered with arithmetic. The teacher picked up a meter stick slowly and thoughtfully, as if she were about to explain it. Instead she whipped its flat side down on her desk with a sharp crack.

"That will be all for you, Mr. Hardaway," she said matter-of-factly, in a surprisingly sweet voice. "You may go to the principal's office. The charming children in this classroom want to learn, and your behavior stands in their way. This I cannot tolerate. Good-bye!"

Mr. Hardaway slunk out of the room.

Mimi zoomed in on Mrs. Krishnamurti's face, which looked rather more pleasant and kindly from close up than at a distance. The trace of a smile played over her features, then vanished as she surveyed the room and saw Emma's empty desk.

Mimi whispered Emma's address in Mrs. Krishnamurti's ear.

Mrs. Krishnamurti frowned and looked again at Emma's desk. She paced aimlessly for a moment, then stopped and set her shoulders as if she had made up her mind about something.

"We've got her," whispered Mimi to the other Muses. "What time does school let out?"

"Three o'clock," said Emma.

They looked at the clock. It was almost three. Mrs. Krishnamurti said a few more baffling math words and then dismissed the class.

A few minutes later she was at Drinkwater's front door. She knocked. The door opened, and there stood Emma's foster father, wearing a dirty shirt and a distracted expression. He stared at the teacher stupidly.

"Mhmmmmnnnghh?" he asked.

"I am Mrs. Krishnamurti, Emma's teacher," the woman replied, "and I'm worried about Emma. She hasn't been to class for over a week—" Feather looked at Emma in surprise. He thought she had only missed the two days in Kokonino County. "And the school's calls haven't been answered. I wonder if Emma's all right?"

Drinkwater's face opened into a false smile, which displayed a number of uneven, speckled teeth. "I'm very pleased to meet you, Mrs. Krish—Krish—"

"Krishnamurti. May I see Emma?"

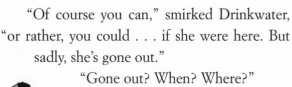

"Of course you can," smirked Drinkwater, "or rather, you could . . . if she were here. But sadly, she's gone out."

"Gone out? When? Where?"

"I don't know, and frankly, I don't care!" replied Drinkwater gleefully.

"Mr. Drinkwater," said the teacher, "Emma has missed a week of school, and you don't know her whereabouts. This is a serious matter. I may be forced to refer it to a truant officer, or even the police."

"The police?" said Drinkwater with alarm. "That shouldn't be necessary! Couldn't we just . . . ah . . . forget the whole thing?"

As Mrs. Krishnamurti thought this over, Mimi whispered in her ear, "Emma's room."

The teacher immediately said, "Perhaps I could come in and look at her room? It may give us some clue."

Drinkwater scowled and tucked in his shirt, flexing his massive, doughy forearms. "I don't know," he started to say, but before he could move, the teacher breezed past him into the house.

"Which room is hers?" she asked.

With surprising quickness, Drinkwater leaped back. He collided with Mrs. Krishnamurti, and she fell hard against the wall. Wincing in pain and holding her right shoulder, she stared up at him. Drinkwater's breath came in heavy gasps as he towered over her in the entryway. His fingers worked convulsively like little, writhing sausages.

"All right. I'll go," said Mrs. Krishnamurti at last in her cool, matter-of-fact way. "But I repeat: I regard this as a very serious matter."

Mimi zoomed in again. "Something from her parents," she said and zoomed out to watch the result.

"Before I go," said Mrs. Krishnamurti, kneading her sore shoulder, "I wonder if you have anything here that might provide a clue to Emma's whereabouts. I know something about the circumstances of her parents' deaths, and I know the girl hasn't got over it yet. Do you have something—anything—from her parents? A photo, a book, a computer disk, a letter? I can't help but think that her disappearance has something to do with her parents, but I don't know where to start."

This line of questions startled the doughy giant. His eyes bulged, then narrowed suspiciously. He looked sideways left and right. He stepped forward. Mrs. Krishnamurti stepped back. He advanced. She retreated, backing toward the front door. She opened it and turned on him bravely.

"I repeat, Mr. Drinkwater, the district will take this situation very seriously indeed. They may need to involve the police."

"AARH!" roared Darien Drinkwater. Up rose his fearsome right arm, its heavy flesh swaying, and his little fist flew at Mrs. Krishnamurti's head. It missed. She jerked to one side, lost her balance, and fell backward down the steps. Her head struck the cement at the bottom with a small crunch, disturbingly quiet. Her body went limp. Drinkwater, a look of horror in his eyes, skipped down after her and scanned the street wildly for witnesses. There seemed to be none. He bent his huge body over her frail form, shielding her from view, and after making sure she was still breathing, he scooped her up as if weightless and carried her into the house.

He hurried down the hall to the cellar door. Breathing heavily, he opened it and carried her down the stairs into an airless, dim, underground room. Mrs. Krishnamurti's head lolled back as he dumped her onto a dusty, yellow sofa. Drinkwater arranged her body into something like a comfortable position, and after scanning the room to make sure everything was in place, he lumbered upstairs, closed the door behind him, and locked it from the outside with a great, blue metal key. The teacher was imprisoned in near total darkness.

Emma shrieked. Her foster father looked around wildly. While the other Muses shushed Emma, Drinkwater muttered to himself, "Nobody here . . . nobody here . . . voices not real . . . the paper, the paper . . . mustn't let the voices see the paper . . ."

"This seems a little extreme," whispered Mimi. "What is *with* this guy?"

The big body on its little feet hurried back to the study. Drinkwater squatted heavily on the floor. He wrestled a small metal safe from under the bed and opened it with a few spins of a combination lock.

"Now!" whispered Mimi to Urania.

With the Muses looking over his shoulder, Emma's foster father rummaged through a jumble of personal belongings—old checkbooks, bank statements, photographs, a few silk handkerchiefs (mementos of his childhood, when he had been an amateur magician)—and at last he produced a greasy piece of paper made by taping two smaller pieces together. Satisfied that it was still there, he replaced the paper, closed the door, spun the dial to lock it again, and wrapping his arms around the safe, hoisted it up with a ferocious grunt.

Staggering under the weight, Drinkwater carried the lockbox to the backyard, where a lovely garden of flowers waved in a riot of yellow daffodils, blue irises, and orange-red freesias. An involuntary peep of appreciation from Feather made Drinkwater look up warily. His jowls vibrated. He squinted. He smiled semitoothlessly. He dropped the safe directly on top of the daffodils. Feather gasped.

The Large, Unpleasant Human (as Feather had begun to think of Mr. Drinkwater) plunged a shovel into the garden soil. The blade sliced mercilessly through stems and petals. Fragments of blue, yellow, orange, and green flew through the air like confetti and settled on the raw earth. Soon not a flower was left standing. In the center of the wasteland gaped a deep hole into which Drinkwater dumped the safe and all its contents.

"NO NO NO NO NO!" screamed Feather. His opinion of Mr. Drinkwater had sunk as deep as this pit.

Drinkwater put his hands to his ears. "The voices! I can't stand the voices!" He leaped back from the safe's grave and, without bothering to refill it with earth, ran into the house, dived into bed, and pulled the covers up over his head. Soon he was snoring.

The Muses looked at each other. After a long silence Urania spoke.

"Nice work, Mimi," she said in her most superior, astronomical voice.

"Don't talk down to me," said Mimi. "I did the best I could. You know how hard it is to do this job with a lot of Muses looking over your shoulder. It's hard enough alone!"

"What are you going to do about Mrs. Krishnamurti?" Emma quavered.

"I don't know," answered Mimi. "Maybe nothing. Are you sure she needs help?"

"And what about that beautiful garden?" Feather was still in shock.

"I'm sure you'll think of something," offered Mimi. "But aren't you forgetting what you came for? You wanted a look at that paper, and I gave it to you. Urania, did you see what it said? Did you copy it down?"

"I didn't have to copy it," said the Muse of Astronomy, "because I memorized it."

"You did? You memorized the message from my parents?" said Emma. "And you'll be able to decode what it means?"

"Maybe," said Urania uncertainly, "but—"

She was interrupted by a loud hissing sound. Smoke filled the room. The Intelligent Air picture winked out. Suddenly they were flooded with light.

Something had dissolved a hole in the roof.

8

Smart Pies

AT EXACTLY THE SAME MOMENT, Feather received an electric jolt that shivered his chin wattles and made him rise from his seat like a kernel of corn jumping in a hot popper.

"What was that?" asked everyone at the same time. All but Feather were looking at the sky through the hole in the ceiling. They seemed not to have noticed his sudden distress. While they continued staring upward, Feather felt a second shock, then a third. He suddenly remembered his mission. Look at Urania, and don't stop. This was the signal. The on switch in his shirt. He began pounding his chest where the button was sewn in, and the electric reminders quit. He gazed steadily at Urania.

She stood trembling directly under the hole, seemingly paralyzed with indecision and fear.

"Quick!" shouted Emma's voice from his left. "Use the umbrella!"

Urania looked startled. With trembling fingers, she opened the leather bag Emma had brought her. From its depths she withdrew a sort of cane. It was unlike any cane Feather had ever seen before, or any umbrella. At one end was a curved leather grip, its crimson color matching Urania's hair ribbon, and at the other end was a sort of knob, or swelling, that seemed to be made of many small parts perfectly fitted together, like the most complicated jigsaw puzzle ever made. Urania stared at the knob.

"Raise it in the air! Push the button!" urged Emma. "And hurry!"

Urania nervously raised the cane above her head. The knob quivered, bulged, and began to unfurl. A wrinkled membrane, crisscrossed with segmented spokes, spread out like a butterfly emerging from its chrysalis. As the spokes straightened into long, slender ribs, the membrane grew taut, smooth, and shiny green, forming a ten-foot-wide circular shield centered directly over Urania's head.

"What is going on here?" moaned Mimi. "What happened to my roof?"

"Get under the umbrella," said Urania. "We're being attacked. Feather is wearing a hidden camera that beams images back to receivers at Chad's lab, where they're stored in memory chips baked into the guidance systems of rocket-powered Smart Pies."

"Smart Pies?" yelped Mimi.

"Yes, they have the ability to aim themselves at whatever they 'see' in their memory. Launched from far away, the pies are guided by satellite until they approach their target. Then they use their intelligence to home in at the end with pinpoint precision. Luckily, I have some protection." Urania nodded at the umbrella over her head.

Feather frowned. How come Urania knew more about what he was doing than he did? And why couldn't he understand a word she said?

Emma and Mimi squeezed under the umbrella just as the first pie hurtled down through the hole in the roof. It blasted into the gossamer shield directly above Urania's head. The thin membrane barely quivered. Pink goo ringed the point of impact, and a trickle of strawberry juice, in dutiful obedience to the law of gravity, oozed toward the umbrella's edge and dripped harmlessly onto the floor.

Feather panicked. He remembered the relentless bombardment at the mall. He stepped away from the broad umbrella. He looked for the exit. He saw the alarmed expression on Mimi's face. He saw a lamp with its shade askew. He saw a discarded Eminem CD. He saw a stain on the wall. He stopped in front of a gilt-framed hanging mirror. He saw himself. His eyes were wild.

A second pie sailed in. It smacked a perfect green bull's-eye on the umbrella directly above Mimi. Key lime, thought Feather, but why was it aiming at Mimi instead of Urania?

A third pie arrived. This one slowed uncertainly as it fell. It hovered briefly just above the big umbrella. It turned this way and that in search of its target, then suddenly roared off sideways and knocked over the table lamp, which crashed to the floor. A fourth pie arrived, pulled up, veered off, and had a messy encounter with the Eminem CD.

Oh no, thought Feather, as the fifth pie smashed into the stain on the wall. Those are all the things I just looked at. And now—he saw his own horrified face in the mirror. He turned away, sprinted to the door, and grasped the handle firmly. He swiveled around for a last look. He knew he would have to describe this scene to Kokopelli. He hoped he had earned his doughnuts. The sixth pie met his face with a lumpy, icy, gravelly *squishbukbukkrunchh* of freezing chocolate, sharp pointy nuts, and—were those marshmallows?

He lay quietly, not knowing if he was asleep or awake. In the distance, as if in a cold, dark dream, he seemed to hear voices.

He heard Emma ask Urania to help decode her message.

He heard Urania say, "Not now, Emma. Kokopelli will strike again. How can I concentrate on math when I have to defend myself?"

Did he hear Emma shouting? Talking to Mimi? Was that a door slamming? It was so far away. . . .

Mimi said something about an umbrella.

Urania said, "What's it made out of, anyway?"

"Rocky road ice cream, I think," murmured Feather just before he blacked out completely.

9

Synthetic Prune Juice

FEATHER VAGUELY WOKE UP. Again he heard voices, different voices.

"Quick! Let's hide him behind this boulder!" It was Kokopelli. "If Urania sees me, she'll kill me!" He laughed. Apparently the idea of having his life ended by an angry Astronomy Muse was not something that worried Kokopelli very much. A second voice began laughing, too.

"What a mess!" it giggled. "Did you have to turn the hose on him like that?"

It was Emma.

"Well, you have to admit it was quick!" Kokopelli again.

Slowly and sleepily, Feather's brain turned over. What did she have to laugh about? Her foster father had done awful things. She had lost the last scrap of paper from her parents. She was depending on Urania to decode its message, but Urania refused to help as long as Kokopelli was flinging pies at her. And now Emma was helping Kokopelli? And laughing? What sense did *that* make?

Maybe, he thought, her misery was an act. Maybe she was only pretending to be sad, so that . . . so that . . . so that she could—what? Who knows? What *was* she trying to do? It made Feather's head hurt. Ow! It really did hurt. Something was steadily scraping the back of his skull. He opened his eyes. He saw the sky. He saw towering rocks. They seemed to be moving. Ah, he thought. That explains it. The ground is scraping my head. No, my head is scraping the ground. I'm being dragged by the heels. Across the desert.

They turned a corner and stopped. Suddenly he was aware of being very wet. He prodded himself with his fingers. No doubt about it. He was soaked and squishy.

Two faces loomed into view: Emma's and Kokopelli's.

"Look at you!" roared the trickster. "You're completely drenched! Good thing I made sure your electronics were waterproof!"

Feather spat out a mouthful of water. "Emma," he asked, "what are you doing here? Aren't you going to stay with Urania while she helps you de—"

Emma interrupted him by clearing her throat with a loud *hrrraf*. "Yes, I *would* be," she said quickly. "It's just that she's kind of *distracted* at the moment. No time to

help *me.* She needs to . . . to work on . . . um . . . Mimi's
house. Do some calculations to . . . ah . . . repair the roof.
Very busy. So I told them not to worry about *you,* because
I could go help you out. It's the least I could do, after all
you've done for me. I'm very sorry you're all wet and
chocolaty. Are you all right?"

"Fine, thank you," he dribbled.

"I ran into Kokopelli just outside the door."

"And I was so delighted she did!" burst in Kokopelli.
"I hope you realize, Feather, that this is one
remarkable Human!" He looked fondly at
Emma, who blushed modestly.

Feather must have looked confused.

"Feather, my Muse," said Kokopelli,
"haven't you ever found someone with such a
great gift for plants that it just makes you drop
your watering can? Someone who raises up
beautiful yams or marigolds or Venus flytraps—or whatever you vegetable people grow—without any help from a
Muse? Someone with such a feel for fruit that all you can
do as a Muse is wallow in worship?"

"No, not really."

"Oh, come *onnnn!* No really great farmers?"

"Well . . . maybe . . ." Feather was having a hard time
thinking at the moment. In that respect, this moment was
no different from other moments.

"For me, that person stands before you," said
Kokopelli, touching Emma's shoulder with his spiky paw.

"She's good with plants?"

"No, no, no, you imbecilic umbilicus, she's a natural-born *trickster!* The one *I* don't have to teach! She's fantastic!" He paused and gazed at her with admiration. "Some of her pranks were an education even for *me.* Do you realize that she once poured rubber cement in the toilet and set it on fire just as her foster father was about to sit down? Talk about *priceless!*" He staggered with laughter and fell on the ground, pounding the sand. Feather looked at Emma. He wondered what else Drinkwater had had to put up with.

"Of course," continued the imp, "as you say, nobody's perfect. She's pulled a few lame ones, too. Like the time she ordered a pizza delivered to—"

"Koko!" said Emma. "You're embarrassing me!"

"Yes, sorry," said Kokopelli. "Anyway, you can understand how delighted I am to meet her. Emma's a special case. A Muse doesn't want to rely on Intelligent Air all the time. Sometimes you need real *face time.*"

Feather shrugged. His stomach muttered impatient reminders. His mind wandered in another direction. He had just guided Kokopelli's Smart Pies, he thought, and now surely, Kokopelli was here to deliver his doughnuts.

"You know," said Kokopelli as if he read Feather's mind, "you'll have to do better next time."

Feather didn't like the sound of this. "Next time?"

"If you want those doughnuts, you'll have to try again."

Kokopelli's meaning was all too clear.

"But I *stared* at Urania," Feather whined. And took a pie in the face and got hosed, too, he added inwardly. I surely deserve *something.*

"You did take a pie in the face and get hosed," Kokopelli said in his uncanny, mind-reading way. "You *do* deserve something."

"Thank you."

"Unfortunately, I don't have anything with me right now except this." He raised the hose in one hand. Feather winced. "And *this.*" Kokopelli raised a gleaming, bright pink glazed doughnut in the other. In a flash, Feather's attention was fully focused.

"Isn't that—ulp—a Very Very Nondairy Strawberry? With raisin glazin'?"

"You have a keen eye for doughnuts, my Muse. Yes, it is. Now, why don't you tell me what happened in there?"

Feather gazed longingly at the doughnut as he wrung out his cloak. Water pooled at his feet. His clothes began to dry in the arid desert air. His mood improved. He described the scene at Mimi's: the dissolving roof, the huge umbrella, the stray pies. Emma confirmed the details and added a few that Feather had missed while he was running around the room. She did, however, fail to mention that she had been the one to bring Urania the umbrella.

"Chad!" muttered Kokopelli.

"Bless you! Are you coming down with something?" asked Feather, thinking, Even though I'm the wet one.

"No, I mean we have to tell this to Chad. Come on,

Emma. Watch how it's done!" Holding the doughnut aloft in one hand and grasping Emma's hand in the other, Kokopelli took off running down the road. Feather

squawked and followed him as fast as his stubby legs would carry him. As they trotted along, Kokopelli soothed Feather by saying how wonderfully *accurate* his description had been, how *important* it would be for the advancement of science, how *much* his help would be needed in case "anything happened," and how *delicious* the latest flavors of Krusty-Glop doughnuts were rumored to be. The Nondairy Strawberry, meanwhile, stayed just out of reach, since Feather could never overtake the swifter and nimbler Muse of Tricks and Tunes. Soon they arrived at Chad's door.

Kokopelli never slowed down. Like a tiny typhoon, he swept Emma straight through the dome and into the lab, where Chad and Aeiou, Muse of Software, sat amid the clutter of tools and spools.

Aeiou was the genius who programmed all Chad's computers. Without her software, his hardware would be useless. She had a small, round head with a small, round face, and her black hair was drawn back in a small, round bun. She wore a high-necked pink gown with extremely long sleeves, the cuffs of which drooped far beyond her hands. These sleeves were Aeiou's only means of communication, since she never spoke, but rather signaled her meaning mutely by waving her arms in complicated patterns in the air.

No one could understand what she was "saying" except for Crraw, a crow who was also, incidentally, the Muse of Bad Poetry, and who now perched on Aeiou's shoulder and translated her sleeve dance. It mystified Feather how the crow could understand sleeves—or how Aeiou could talk about software with sleeves, or type at a keyboard through sleeves, for that matter.

At the moment, the Muse of Software was twirling the dial on an Intelligent Air terminal—colored the same pink as her dress—and watching the image of a worried-looking girl sitting at a computer. Its monitor displayed a bomb icon and the message "Please Restart Your Bartlett." The girl was frantically punching her keyboard, but no matter which combination of buttons she typed, the screen refused to change. Her Bartlett was frozen.

Aeiou signaled an elaborate semaphore with her sleeves, and Crraw translated. "Aeiou says she has quite a few programs running at once—IM-ing, playing a DVD, working on a school paper in NanoSoft Verbiage, and editing images from her digital camera."

"Yes," Chad replied, "but she has plenty of RAM, so why should—"

Aeiou interrupted him with another sleeve dance. Crraw said, "Aeiou says there may be a conflict between IMs, TSR, and the PROM's USB IOS, which . . ." He went on for some minutes in this opaque vein.

"In that case," said Chad, "we should tell her to—"

"Whack it with your shoe!" shouted Kokopelli.

The girl's expression brightened. She slipped off one of her sandals and began beating her computer with it.

"Stop! Stop!" said Chad, but the girl wasn't listening. She looked very, very happy.

To everyone's amazement, the computer restarted.

"Hey!" growled Kokopelli. "That wasn't supposed to work!"

Aeiou spun the dial, and the picture winked out. "We'll take a look at this later," said Chad. He and Aeiou eyed the other three silently. Feather looked sideways at Emma. She seemed to be perfectly happy.

"Does anyone here know anything about a TEN-FOOT-WIDE PIE-PROOF UMBRELLA?" bellowed Kokopelli.

Chad smiled. "Ah!" he said cheerfully. "Sit down. Would you like a glass of synthetic prune juice? Made entirely from recycled plastic electrical insulation, but I think you'll agree it's close enough to the real thing." Aeiou held out three glasses of brownish, oily-looking liquid on a tray.

"Thank you, Aeiou." Feather took a sip. Not bad. Sweet. At first. A bit plasticky going down, though, with a hint of burning tires. He looked discreetly for someplace to set down his glass. And something to wash the taste from his mouth. A pink doughnut would do nicely, he thought, but the only one in sight still hovered high above Kokopelli's head.

"Ten-foot-wide pie-proof umbrella," the imp repeated through clenched teeth, if he had teeth. It was hard to tell. Kokopelli's features were so shadowy. He was nothing but a silhouette really, a dangerous, untrustworthy silhouette. Chad coughed and looked at Aeiou, who made a sort of shrug. Feather thought she may have been warning him off the prune juice.

"The problem of pie defense is something that interests me, yes," said Chad coolly.

"Go on," said Kokopelli.

"After a good deal of trial and error, guessing and stressing and messing about—you'd probably call it the 'scientific method'—I was able to invent a wonderful new clothlike material, ultrastrong, but so thin that acres of it can be folded up into a slender wand. It's completely impervious to pies. I call it 'chadium.'"

"How MODEST of you!" Kokopelli yelled. "And would you like to tell me how you expect me to— How I'm supposed to— How I can possibly—no, no, no— How WE can expect to deliver a Smart Pie to Urania's face, if YOU keep figuring out ways to STOP it?!"

"Another very interesting problem. And I may have solved this one as well. The idea is so simple, I don't know why I didn't think of it sooner!"

"And that idea is . . . ?"

"USE SMARTER PIES."

"Smarter Pies?" Kokopelli began to sound hopeful again.

"I've been experimenting with ways to pierce or avoid a chadium shield. Aeiou has just been helping me analyze the results, and I must say they are most encouraging."

"Encouraging you *can* pierce it, or encouraging you *can't?*"

"A little of each."

"You're saying you may have some way to get through that ten-foot umbrella?"

"Or around it."

"And you're willing to try it out?"

"I don't see the point of developing something without testing it." Chad explained his ideas. Feather missed most of it, especially since throughout the talk Kokopelli insisted on playing his flute at top volume with one hand while waving the doughnut around with the other, but he got the impression that Smarter Pies could sense and steer around chadium barriers, that the extra sensors and rocket motors required would add a little heft to the pies—they'd be three feet wide, weigh thirty-eight pounds each, be bristling with metal, and there would be plenty of them—and that it was more important than ever that you KEEP YOUR EYES ON URANIA THIS TIME BECAUSE WE DON'T WANT TO MISS.

Chad stopped and invited questions.

Emma asked, "Isn't thirty-eight pounds a lot of pie to drop on somebody?" To Feather, she sounded less concerned than you might expect from someone whose only hope for deliverance was about to be slammed with an avalanche of creamed metal.

Kokopelli snorted. "If you want to learn from the master, don't ask questions!"

"Sorry," replied Emma meekly, though Feather could tell she was annoyed.

"The important question, Obi-Chad, genius of the universe," continued Kokopelli, "is, do you know of *any way* these Smarter Pies can be stopped?"

"Not yet I don't," said Chad.

"Well, if you do figure one out, will you PLEASE keep it from falling into the wrong hands?" A strange expression, thought Feather. Hands could be either right or left. But wrong? Which hands were wrong? He tried to remember if any of the Muses were left-handed.

"I promise," said Chad.

"To do what?" asked Kokopelli.

"Absolutely everything I can."

"Well, then, let's get moving!"

"Where's my doughnut?" asked Feather.

The glistening, pink confection seemed to have disappeared. How did he *do* that?

"Don't look so glum, Feather!" shouted Kokopelli far too cheerfully. "We're *this* close now—and you know what that means!"

Feather nodded glumly. He knew *what* it meant, but he didn't know *when.* How long would he have to stare at Urania before he got his doughnuts?

Kokopelli asked the scientists how long the Smarter Pie system would take to program and build. The question plunged Chad and Aeiou into a heated technical discussion, which involved Chad uttering long-winded paragraphs of incomprehensible gibberish and Aeiou twirling and flipping her sleeves, gestures that Crraw, the crow, interpreted in his own long-winded paragraphs. While Crraw talked, Aeiou typed furiously at the computer keyboard. Emma watched entranced. Kokopelli noodled and toodled. Feather took another sip of artificial prune juice. Not bad.

Just as he was about to ask for seconds, the Muses of Hardware and Software came to an agreement. The Smarter Pies, they said, would be ready next Tuesday. As it was now only last Wednesday, Feather's face fell and his stomach howled so loudly that the other Muses actually looked frightened for a moment, until they realized what it was. So it was hardly surprising that no one seemed sorry when he pointedly announced that he was going home for some *broccoli pie.* He looked wistfully at Emma, hoping she would keep him company—he was growing attached to this Human—but she was clearly having too much fun to tear herself away.

Sadly, Feather—and his stomach—took their leave.

Back at his kitchen table, as he munched his broccoli pie with brown-fried onions—a satisfying though hardly thrilling meal—just one thought filled his mind:

A week was a long time to wait.

10

Drinkwater's
Basement

EMMA SPENT MOST of the next week with Chad and Aeiou. This was odd. Why wasn't she talking to Urania? That message needed decoding! But instead of taking care of business, the girl seemed to be wasting all her time in the lab. Sometimes she took breaks, but only to visit Kokopelli for—who knows what? Feather could hear their snorts and chortles echoing off the desert rocks. It was all so very confusing. Confusing and disturbing.

Even more disturbing, Emma never asked about her foster father, Mr. Drinkwater, or her teacher, Mrs. Krishnamurti, now a prisoner in Drinkwater's basement. And most disturbing of all (to Feather), she seemed not to care about her ruined garden. That garden!

Feather spun the dial on his Intelligent Air tangerine. Soon Drinkwater's backyard came into view. All signs of life had disappeared. It looked dusty and flat and very tightly packed, as if an angry giant had spanked it with the flat of a shovel. Drinkwater must have filled in the hole and tamped down the earth. Feather sighed. How could this . . . this . . . *plant vandal* be helped?

He began looking for Drinkwater inside the house. He searched the bedrooms, the living room, the kitchen, and the hall, still dusty and littered with broken glass. He even peeked into the bathroom. (Muses do that more often than you might think!) Where was the Human?

There was a slight movement in the hall. A half-open door creaked in the breeze. Feather looked through the narrow opening and saw the basement stairs. In the dim light, an elephantine shadow loomed on the wall. A harsh voice echoed up the stairwell.

"I'm sorry, Mrs. Krishnamurti," Drinkwater was saying in a tone both reasonable and creepy, "but I honestly can't make up my mind. On the one hand, I want to do the right thing and let you go. On the other hand, if I let you go—you still intend to call the police?"

"Of course," replied Mrs. Krishnamurti evenly. She looked gaunt and hungry. Her cheeks were hollow and dark, and her eyes glowed in their sockets.

Drinkwater sighed. "It's a tragedy, really, what's happening to me."

"To *you?*"

"Bad things keep happening," he sniffed, "and I can't seem to help it. I never wanted to lose anyone, or drive anyone away, or hurt anyone—" He waved his hand at Mrs. Krishnamurti. "But it just happens. What an awful fate is mine!" He moaned with self-pity. "I didn't tell you to come meddling in my business, did I? But you did, and here you are. Is that *my* fault?"

"If you don't let me go, things will be even worse for you," pointed out the teacher, not unreasonably.

"Not necessarily, my dear, not necessarily at all! Darien Drinkwater knows how to protect himself! He knows how to hide things so they're never found out! Yes, indeed he does, indeed he does. . . ."

"*What* are you talking about?" said Mrs. Krishnamurti.

The safe, thought Feather, but he's wrong. *We* know about it.

"Never mind!" said the doughy giant, waving a tiny paw. "I'll figure it out for myself; I always do. And I'd better do it soon. You're costing me sandwich money!" He tossed a packet on the table. "Here's today's! I hope you like roast beef!"

In the weak light, which filtered in from a small barred window high on one wall, Feather could see a number of half-eaten sandwiches scattered over the table. They were not half-eaten in the usual way, from the edge, but rather from the top and bottom toward the filling, as if Mrs. Krishnamurti had nibbled only the bread.

"I never touch beef," she said.

Ants swarmed hungrily over the leavings. Apparently Mrs. Krishnamurti also did not believe in killing ants.

As Feather watched, a curious expression stole over the teacher's face. A sly expression. A hopeful expression. Feather knew that expression. It was the expression of someone having an idea. One of the other Muses must be whispering to Mrs. Krishnamurti!

"I wonder," said Mrs. Krishnamurti. "Since I will probably be down here some time, can you do me a small small favor?"

"Mmmnnngh?"

"I wonder if you could bring me something to pass the time? It gets so terribly boring without radio or television or DVD. But I am a lover of crossword puzzles. It would make me so happy to have the newspaper and a pen. Many newspapers, actually. Then I could do my crosswords morning, noon, and night. What could be more pleasant?" She looked at him brightly.

He stared at her blankly for a few moments. "You do your crossword puzzles in pen?" he said at last. He sounded impressed.

"Yes, I think it's much *braver* in pen, don't you?"

Drinkwater clearly had no opinion.

"Well, may I have my crosswords or not?"

"Well . . . I don't see why not. . . ."

"Then get along with you, man! Why wait? I have a long afternoon ahead of me! Is there any reason I can't start right away?"

Drinkwater mumbled something, turned, and heaved himself with much effort up the stairs. In a few minutes, he returned with a stack of old newspapers, which he dumped on the floor at her feet. He handed her a ballpoint pen. Then, without a word, he left. The stairs creaked under his weight. Feather heard the door slam and the sound of several keys turning in locks. Again, Mrs. Krishnamurti was alone.

She bent down and peeled off one sheet of newspaper. Holding this single thickness of paper aloft in front of her, she began tearing it lengthwise into narrow strips. The paper tore neatly and easily in nearly straight lines, and soon a pile of thin paper ribbons lay at Mrs. Krishnamurti's feet.

She picked up three strips of paper. She pinched them together at one end so they hung side by side, three shreds of exactly equal length. Then she began to braid them.

How boring, thought Feather. He clicked off his terminal, and the image of Mrs. Krishnamurti disappeared.

11

Smarter Pies

AT LAST TUESDAY CAME. Second or third thing in the morning, at around half past eleven, Feather knocked on Mimi's door. (He had meant to be there first thing in the morning, at nine o'clock sharp, but he overslept.) Feather knew he would find Urania at Mimi's. Ever since the Smart Pie attack, Urania had been helping to repair the damage and clean up the mess. As well she might, he thought irritably. It had been partly her fault, hadn't it? Nobody *forced* her to be at Mimi's when the rain of pies began. Feather's annoyance mounted. He wondered whether he would ever see doughnuts again. He stamped his feet impatiently, or tried to, but they were stuck to the porch by a week-old film of melted rocky road ice cream. He shifted his weight from foot to foot with a *squinch, squinch, squinch.*

The door opened. There stood Aeiou, Muse of Software. Odd. What was she doing here? She was supposed to be working with Chad on the pies, not visiting the target. Feather was so befuddled that he barely noticed the Muse of Software's elaborate sleeve dance. Her cuffs skated forward and back, snapping and gliding, while her feet in their platform clogs shuffled and tapped. After some minutes she stopped, and Crraw, hovering nearby as usual, spoke for her.

"Aeiou says hello."

Feather just stared.

Aeiou wiggled, and Crraw translated. "Aeiou says she came to help Mimi fix and clean up her house. Repairs take careful planning, and Aeiou is—"

"A fantastic planner!" Mimi, appearing at the door behind Aeiou, finished the sentence gleefully. "I can't tell you how much easier the work has been with her help! She's so orderly! So systematic! Without her, it would have taken me *years* to clean up. She's just *wonderful!*"

"Ahh . . . is Urania here?" asked Feather.

"Oh yes!" said Mimi. "She's doing all the calculations: how much soap to add to the cleaning water, how many boards, nails, shingles, and all that. It's wonderful how much gets done when Muses work together!" Feather wondered ungenerously exactly what job Mimi herself was doing—probably spinning CDs and eating those ghastly frozen toaster pies while the others slaved away.

He stood on tiptoe and craned his neck to see inside, but his eyes barely came up to the level of Aeiou's shoulder. Why did these particular Muses have to be so *tall?* Was *anybody* going to invite him in? Was he supposed to stand here all *day?* He decided to risk rudeness and come straight to the point.

"May I come in?" he asked.

"Oh, I don't think that would be a very good idea," said Mimi dryly. She pointed at a jagged outcropping of boulders some hundred yards away. "Go sit on those rocks. We'll be out in a minute. And stop looking at me!"

Feather briefly considered trying to force his way in. But there were three of them, and they were so big. Well, if they would come to him, he could wait. But not for long! If they delayed and left him sitting stupidly outside, he would . . . he would . . . think of something, probably. He waddled over to the rocks, climbed up, and sat down on them with his legs tucked under him.

From this distance the house looked like a dollhouse under construction. Evidence of repair was everywhere. The roof gleamed with new shingles, and lumber lay in tidy piles by the door.

Soon the four Muses (including Crraw) emerged. Aeiou, Mimi, and Urania marched in close formation like a military unit, quick, serious, and purposeful. Well, Feather thought, I can be serious and purposeful, too.

He boldly pressed the button under his shirt to activate the camera and began staring at Urania with big, innocent eyes.

"Feather," said Mimi.

"Mimi," said Feather.

"Will you look at me when I speak to you?" said Mimi.

"No," replied Feather, looking sideways squarely at Urania's face.

"We want you to take this letter to Kokopelli. Right away."

Out of the corner of his eye, he saw Urania produce something from the folds of her robe and extend it toward him. Don't look down, he thought.

Feather extended his hand blindly. His fingers crunched end-on into something hard. His eyes watered, but with a great effort he kept them open. Urania gently took his hand and folded his throbbing fingers around what felt like an envelope.

"Off you go, then!" said Mimi. "Right away! What are you waiting for?"

Pineapple Pumpkin Sweet-Potato Puffs, he thought. Chocolate Churros. The deep-fried stuff that dreams are made of. That's what I'm waiting for. I'm going to stay until this job is done, and done right.

Feather heard beeping. It seemed to come from Urania's staff. Without hesitation, the Muse of Astronomy raised it high in the air, and Feather thought, Go ahead. Nice try. This time I'm staying put. See what your chadium umbrella can do for you now.

But there was no chadium umbrella. Instead of unfurling as before, Urania's wand began to sprout transparent branches like twigs on a flexible glass tree. These filaments writhed like snakes, guided by some unseen mechanism in the base of the wand. From their tips, brilliant, ruby-red lines of laser light beamed into the sky.

Far above their heads came a faint sound. *Pof pof pof pof pof.* Then silence.

"Aeiou says you got them all," said Crraw. Urania lowered her wand. The glassy branches were gone.

"Wh-what just happened?" asked Feather.

"Aeiou says that all the Smarter Pies have been vaporized," explained Crraw. Tiny metallic flakes of whipped-cream-covered tinsel began settling harmlessly all around them. Apparently, this was all that was left of the hefty missiles.

"Off you go, then, Feather," said Urania, giving him a gentle push.

The attack of the Smarter Pies was over? Feather's spirits rose. How easy! He wanted to shout for joy and cry with relief. He had done exactly what he was supposed to do, and no one had been hurt. Urania would finally be able to help Emma. Above all, doughnuts would now be his!

He took his eyes off Urania's face and looked at the other Muses gratefully. Somehow, they seemed to be holding a tuba, a drum, and a piccolo. The tuba bore a faint hollow where Feather's fingers had dented it when he reached for the letter. The band struck up the theme from *Star Wars*.

As Feather sped gleefully away toward Kokopelli's, several questions nagged at his mind: Where was Emma? Was Urania finally ready to help her? Would the doughnuts still be fresh after all this time? And what was in that letter?

12

A Letter

ADMIT IT: if you were Feather, you would have read Urania's letter, too, especially since the envelope was unsealed. It opened with no effort at all. In fact, it seemed almost to spring open and read itself. Here is what it said:

Dear Kokopelli,

I miss you. Ever since the last Astronomy Night, things have been different between us. You seem so hostile now. I never see you anymore. I know you're avoiding me.

This makes me terribly sad. You are my favorite Muse. You have so many wonderful qualities. You play beautiful tunes on your flute. You have a great sense of humor. You are witty, intelligent, lively, and cute. You are always true to yourself.

To me, you are the center of the Muse Universe. All of us revolve around you like planets, comets, and asteroids held in orbit by an irresistible gravitational force. Without you, Kokonino County would be a wasteland, a place so dull I would pack my wand and hop a rocket to Neptune, where I could pass the frozen nights staring at the heavens and dreaming of you, my lost Muse.

Sometimes, dear Koko, you seem like an emotional black hole, emitting nothing (except for an occasional pie, which quantum theory leads us to expect). You rarely say how you feel. And then, when you do express yourself, as you did last Astronomy Night, you seem so upset afterward. You wanted to take back your words. You were full of explosive regret.

Ever since then, you've been trying to bomb me with pies. Do you really think this will make me forget what we had together? Do you really feel the need to keep me at a distance this way?

Can't we put these problems behind us? Please, I beg you, come to the observatory tonight. Let's make a new start on a new Astronomy Night. Let me tell you face to face how <u>cosmically great</u> I think you are. And I hope you can tell me your feelings as well, instead of going on with this pointless, futile, mechanical pie-flinging, which threatens not only the Muses, but also Human civilization. I believe you can learn to speak your feelings as wonderfully as you do everything else. I know you can change, because wherever I look in the universe, I see change.

I'm looking forward to a new era of friendship with you, my friend, my Muse, my shining star. See you tonight?

With warmest regards,
Urania

Feather's feathers shivered. Surely this explained everything! Didn't it? It seemed so terribly meaningful, if only he could see what the meaning was. Urania was in love with Kokopelli! Wasn't she? Or was she . . . ? A second reading seemed to raise as many questions as it answered. What had Kokopelli told Urania? How did she respond? What's a gravitational force? He stood scratching his beak for a long time.

"Whatcha got there?" came a voice from over his shoulder. Kokopelli! How did he *do* that?

Feather frantically smushed the letter back into the envelope, trying to shield it with his body from Kokopelli's eyes. Luckily, he had a wide body.

"Eee, bdee, bdum . . . ," he said.

"I *said*, whatcha got there? 'S'matter, cat got your tongue?"

Feather looked down his beak and reached for his tongue. Everything seemed to be in place.

"No, no cat," he replied.

Kokopelli snatched the letter from Feather's hand, opened the envelope, unfolded the letter, and began to read. Soon his little silhouette of a body was trembling with rage, or frustration, or fear, or some disturbing combination of all three. His feet stamped the desert floor, kicking up geysers of sand and dust. His hair snapped like lightning bolts. Cats yowled and coyotes shrieked in the distance. Feather nervously took a step backward, then another. Maybe there was a better time to talk about his doughnuts.

"TALK?" shrieked the trickster. "About FEEL-INGS? I HATE to talk about feelings! But you tell her I'll be there."

"Good! See you tonight!" replied Feather, who didn't stop running until he reached his house.

1 3

Escape Attempt

BACK IN HIS HUT, Feather munched at a large bowl of coleslaw and mused. How much damage, he wondered, would this pie war do to Humanity? It had certainly kept his eyes off the plant world. He could think of several important agricultural problems he had ignored while staring at Urania, and she was even more distracted than he was, without even enough time to help Emma with her little math problem. Then multiply Emma by . . . by . . . by a zillion (Feather was not too clear on large numbers), and there you had it. Probably nobody anywhere had solved a hard math problem in over a week. Could this be a good thing? Feather suspected not. And how much longer would it go on?

"It won't be much longer, Feather, old friend," said a

voice over his shoulder. Kokopelli! How did he *do* that? No—not Kokopelli at all. It was Emma.

"It won't?"

"No. If everything goes according to plan," said the girl, "I should be leaving you soon. I've just come to, um, thank you for everything. You've been a wonderful host." She gave him a kiss on the cheek.

Feather blushed a deep orange and modestly shrugged off the compliment. What plan? he wondered.

"By the way," Emma added, "could you do me a little favor?"

"Only if it's about plants." Feather sighed. "I don't have much luck with anything else."

"Yes, yes. I wonder if you could look in on Mrs. Krishnamurti, in my foster father's basement. I'm worried she's not getting enough to eat. She's a strict vegetarian, you know, and *Drinkwater,*" she pronounced the name as if she were spitting nails, "keeps giving her roast beef sandwiches. Couldn't you help her find some other kind of food down there? Aren't there edible mushrooms, or something else that grows in the dark?"

Of course she was right, Feather thought with embarrassment. Why hadn't he thought of this? He quickly activated his Intelligent Air terminal. As he twirled the dials, he looked at the girl. The sadness in her eyes, so striking the first time he saw her, had given way to pure determination. The Muses, he thought with satisfaction, had helped *this* Human in some way, even if her parents' message was still in code, impossible to understand.

Together they looked at the image of Drinkwater's basement.

Something about the room was different. The pile of sandwich leavings was bigger, and Mrs. Krishnamurti was thinner, and the light was dimmer, and the sofa was dirtier. The sofa had also moved across the room, and the pile of newspapers was gone. The sofa now stood against the wall, under the high, barred window. In place of the newspapers was something that looked like a ragged coil of rope. Mrs. Krishnamurti was busy, still braiding strips of newsprint. When she finished one braid, she wound it together with two other braids, making a thicker strand, which she then wove together with similar strands to make a stout cable several feet long.

She picked up the cable and, with her frail hands, tugged on it as hard as she could. It held fast. With a satisfied look, she set down the rope and picked up the pen she was supposed to be using for crossword puzzles. The pen was chipped and dusty-looking. Holding the pen tightly, Mrs. Krishnamurti climbed unsteadily onto the back of the sofa, stretched up toward the window, and began attacking the plaster on the sill around the base of one of the bars. Feather and Emma watched entranced as she chipped and chipped and chipped some more. Plaster dust and putty and shards of brick crumbled onto the sill and fell onto the back of the sofa and the floor. From time to time, the prisoner would interrupt her work to listen, in case Drinkwater should be coming down the stairs.

She gave a tug on the bar. It moved slightly. She climbed down. She carefully swept up the dust and debris with her hands and brushed it under the sofa. She smiled.

"Chad," whispered Feather to Emma. "Chad gave her this idea, didn't he?"

Emma nodded gravely. "If only—," she started to say, but fell silent when she saw Mrs. Krishnamurti go back to work.

The teacher again climbed onto the sofa. This time she was carrying one end of her handmade rope. She wound several turns of it around the metal bar across the window and tied it off with a tough-looking knot.

She climbed down. She picked up the other end of the rope and carried it across the room to the opposite wall, where a tall filing cabinet stood like a boxy gray sentinel. She pulled the rope tight. Its end stopped just short of the filing cabinet. With her free hand she rolled out the top drawer of the cabinet toward the rope. The cabinet, unbalanced by the long, heavy drawer sticking out (it was full of Drinkwater's unpublished novels), tipped forward suddenly. Mrs. Krishnamurti quickly rolled the drawer back in. The cabinet teetered and righted itself. The teacher put her hand over her heart and panted softly.

She set down the rope. She put her arms around the

filing cabinet. With a surprisingly loud, deep grunt—it sounded like a professional wrestler in an echo chamber—Mrs. Krishnamurti tugged and shoved and spun the massive piece of furniture until it had moved about two feet. Again she pulled out the top drawer—more carefully this time, and only halfway—and satisfied herself that the rope was now within reach. She tied its free end tightly to the handle of the filing cabinet drawer. The other end, of course, was attached to the bar across the window on the other side of the room.

Suddenly, Mrs. Krishnamurti slammed the file drawer shut.

The rope went taut. It yanked the bar. They heard a ripping, grinding noise. The bar popped loose from the window sill and flew through the air straight toward Mrs. Krishnamurti. It clunked against her skull. Feather and Emma both gasped. Mrs. Krishnamurti fell down. The filing cabinet drawer, having slammed shut, bounced open again. As they watched in horror, the drawer slowly rolled out until fully extended. The tall, unbalanced cabinet teetered, tipped, and fell over with a loud crash onto Mrs. Krishnamurti. She was unconscious, pinned beneath the giant metal box.

"WHAZZAT?" Even up a flight of stairs and through the basement door, Drinkwater's yell was as loud as a trumpeting elephant.

"Oh, dear," moaned Emma. "I was afraid of this. I just *knew* Chad was too busy smartening up his pies to work this out right! What a horrible mistake! Oh, dear. Oh NO!"

Just then, Drinkwater rumbled down the stairs into view. He was roaring. Blotches rose on his pasty face like blue, red, and orange lights blinking in a video game.

"Crossword puzzles?" he sneered. "CROSSWORD PUZZLES? So you thought you could make a fool out of Darien Drinkwater, did you? Play a little game with my mind, eh? AAARGH!" he bellowed. "I HATE dishonest people!"

He began muttering to himself. His bristly brows knitted, and his hand began thoughtfully scraping the lumps on his face. "This sinks it, of course . . . can't let her go . . . gotta do away with the . . . nothing else to do . . . but how . . . ? How? How? Hmmmmmmm . . ." His humming was as rough as a diesel engine.

"How about poison?" suggested Feather helpfully.

"Shhhhh!" hissed Emma. "What are you saying?"

"I know some very nice plant-based poisons," Feather whispered back to her. "It's my duty to help people with plant problems." Emma stared at him in disbelief.

Drinkwater's eyes lit up. "Yes . . ." He grinned, showing several teeth like uneven, brown tent pegs. "Poison. Excellent idea! Now, where can I find a poison recipe?"

"The public li—," began Feather, before Emma clamped his beak shut between her hands.

"Stop it!" she growled.

"But I'm supposed to help people," Feather tried to

say, although it came out more like "Bt m spps dhlp ppl," to which he added, "Ld 'o uv m bk," by which he meant, "Let go of my beak."

"Only if you promise to *be quiet.*"

"Ynnrgh! Prms."

She released his beak and glared at the Muse of Plants. He looked at her in bewilderment. This was what happened when you associated with Humans. They took you out of your Muse routine. They played on your sympathies. They interfered with your work by making you take sides. No wonder Muses tried not to get too involved with them.

"Listen, Feather," said Emma, "there's only one thing you can do to help now."

"There is?"

"Yes. The most important thing right now is for you to come to Chad's observatory as soon as possible. You need to be there when Kokopelli meets Urania."

"I do?"

"Yes. There's no time to explain. The sooner we go there the better."

They were interrupted by a roar from Mr. Drinkwater. "YESS!" he crowed, like a baritone rooster. "The public library! They'll have something! Or if not them, then the university library! What wonderful resources! I love libraries! Now, where did I put my library card . . . ?" His little hands fluttered through his pockets like nervous birds. "Must be upstairs . . . well, my dear," he said, addressing the graceful, unconscious form of Mrs. Krishnamurti, "you just stay put under the furniture. Don't want you going anywhere, do we? It might be a little uncomfortable," he gave the cabinet a ferocious kick, "but don't worry. I won't be gone long!"

With that, he huffed up the stairs.

Feather clicked off the Intelligent Air terminal. The image evaporated. Emma took him by the hand and pulled him toward the door.

"Hurry up, Feather!" she whimpered. "We need your eyes!"

What, he wondered, could she possibly mean by that?

1 4

Kokopelli on Trial

FEATHER AND EMMA ARRIVED at the observatory dome just after sunset. The desert's heat was rapidly giving way to a nighttime chill as the sunbaked sand threw back its stored warmth to the empty, insatiable sky. Feather was fairly empty himself. He and the Human had dashed out of the house without eating dinner, and now his stomach was growling again, but quietly, in a voice no louder than an angry kitten's.

As dusk deepened to eggplant black, and stars and planets began to appear from wherever they hide during the day, the two visitors (or three, if you counted Feather's stomach) entered the dome. They were the first to arrive. In the dim light, they could make out the shape of the great telescope. To pass the time, Feather decided to have a look.

Stepping carefully around the heaps of junk—ouch! not carefully enough—he brought his eye to the eyepiece.

He sighed. How disappointing! There was the familiar golden ring again, glowing against the black backdrop of space. The telescope was still tracking the Doughnut of Saturn, just as before. This was hardly surprising. Urania must have been too busy to change any settings.

Feather idly twirled the dial on his Intelligent Air terminal, which he always carried in his pocket just in case. As Emma fidgeted with impatience, he wandered the world, solving plant problems. He pointed out some ripe blackberries to a girl walking in the woods. He told a gardener to put mulch on his cucumber beds. He had a long conversation with a farmer about genetically engineered soybeans. Life can be full, even when your stomach is empty.

His musing was interrupted by a murmur of voices as the other Muses began to arrive. Feather clicked off his terminal and dropped it back into his pocket. Urania entered first, touched a switch, and the lights came up. Seven figures filed in, chatting and milling about: Chad, Urania, Aeiou, Mimi, Crraw, and two other Muses who have had no part in this story: Bo, a cow who is Muse of Miscellaneous Facts, and the little Egyptian Pwt, Muse of Animals. Chad, his flowing white robe belted with a brilliant orange sash, offered glasses of synthetic prune juice all around, which his guests politely accepted and pretended to sip.

Feather heard the sound of flute music. All conversation stopped.

Kokopelli entered. The trembling trickster scanned the room. He seemed on the verge of exploding, or fleeing, or both.

"I see you brought a crowd, Urania," he muttered in a voice loaded with emotions.

"Everyone's welcome at Astronomy Night!" chirped Urania.

"Yes," said the imp. "I'm not really surprised. But I had hoped . . ."

"To see me alone?"

"Never mind."

"It's all right, Kokopelli," she said. "We can talk in front of the others. I have no secrets from any Muse."

"You DON'T?" Koko was aghast. "I have secrets from ALL of them! What's the point of *living* without secrets? Without secrets, how can I play tricks? Without secrets, how can I be *me?*"

Urania rolled her eyes. Mimi spoke up. "Are you saying you don't want to talk?"

"Not in front of this bunch," he said, glaring.

"But we *have* to!" cried Urania.

"No," said Kokopelli.

"Show him the telescope," said Mimi.

Urania took the reluctant Muse of Tricks by the elbow and coaxed him through the throng, which parted like a herd of nervous antelopes before a rabid hyena. When they reached the telescope, Kokopelli hung back.

"Go ahead," said Urania. "Take a look. It can't hurt."

Kokopelli trembled. "Are you sure?"

At last, after much hesitation, Kokopelli bent his eye to the lens. He jumped as if he'd touched a live wire. Something about the view of Saturn made him swallow so hard that everyone could hear the sound echoing around the dome. *Glup glup glup glup glup.* Every part of him drooped.

"All right," he said at last. "I'll talk."

Mimi pushed a chair at the back of his knees, and the deflated trickster collapsed into a limp sitting position.

"Is it true, Kokopelli," began Mimi in a lawyerly voice that Feather had never heard her use before, "that you came to the last Astronomy Night?"

"Yes," he bleated meekly.

"And did you look through the telescope at that time?"

"I did."

"Can you tell us in your own words what you saw?"

"I dunno. Stars. Planets. Galaxies. The Depths of the Universe."

"And did you have some conversation with Urania afterward?"

Kokopelli squirmed. "Do I have to answer that question?"

"YES!" chorused six voices— everyone, that is, except Aeiou, who never spoke, and Feather, who had no opinion, and of course Kokopelli himself. Feather's stomach, however, rumbled like distant thunder.

"We may have talked."

"What did you say to her?"

"I dunno. Stuff. I forget."

Mimi now turned to Urania and asked if she remembered a conversation with Kokopelli on the evening in question. Yes, said Urania, she remembered it clearly. And what did he say at that time?

"He made, I would say, a kind of confession. He admitted that staring into space made him question his life. Seeing the Depths of the Universe made him feel shallow by comparison. Sometimes, he said, he thought his life had no meaning. He wondered what the point was of playing tricks on everyone. Sometimes he thought it would be easier on all of us, including himself, if he gave up his pranks, his insults, and his pie-throwing to become a more pleasant, helpful, and cooperative Muse."

Everyone gasped. Urania stopped. Mimi held back her next question for dramatic effect. In the silence, Feather heard Bo, the cow, whisper to Pwt, "I stare into space all the time, and it never made me question my life," and Pwt whisper back, "But you're a cow."

At last, Mimi turned to Kokopelli. "Is that what you said to Urania?"

Kokopelli's voice could barely be heard. "Something like that."

"And afterward, were you sorry you said it?"

Kokopelli's head sank to his chest.

"*Were you?*"

No answer.

"You thought you had let yourself appear WEAK and VULNERABLE, isn't that true?"

Kokopelli barely nodded.

"You were *afraid* the Muses would think you're a *wimp,* weren't you? A *weakling,* a *pushover,* a *punk?*"

Kokopelli didn't move.

"So you decided to prove to Urania that you were really STRONG—not just prove it to Urania, but to yourself! You pretended you'd never meant any of it! You hatched a diabolical plan to rain down pies on her without regard for others, any place, any time. Isn't that so?"

"Yeah."

Feather wondered how Mimi knew all this. She went on.

"And you enlisted the help of your friends," she waved her arm at Chad, Aeiou, and Feather, "to support your fiendish plot? And they built the machinery and wrote the software and aimed the camera for you?"

The imp looked mildly irritated. "Well, they seemed happy enough to help."

"And do you *really* think that using orbiting satellites to direct remote-controlled Smart Pies is the *best way to deal with your feelings?*"

Kokopelli stiffened ever so slightly. "Oh, I don't know. It looked that way at the time!"

Everyone gasped.

Surprised by this resistance, Mimi paused and collected herself. She smoothed the wrinkles in her costume, which had gotten rather bunchy from her arm-waving and pacing. She took a sip of "prune juice." At last, she began again, her voice dropping dramatically low. Everyone strained to hear.

"Do you promise, Kokopelli," she said, "never to do it again?"

Kokopelli shifted in his seat. He looked around, as if wondering what help to expect from Chad, Aeiou, and Feather. At last, he turned to Urania.

"Look here, Urania," he practically whined. "I admit what I said. I admit what I did. Isn't it your turn to talk now? I didn't just come here to talk. I want to hear *you.* Your letter was full of the most accurate praise of me. You showed you really understand me. And you promised to say more. Isn't it time for you to tell me again how *wonderful* I am?"

Urania blushed. "Um . . . what did I say in that letter, exactly?" she asked Mimi.

"What do you mean?" said Kokopelli wildly. "You wrote it!"

"As a matter of fact," said Urania, "I didn't."

15

The Smartest Pie

"WHAT?" BELLOWED KOKOPELLI. "If you didn't write it, who DID?"

All the Muses began discussing this question at once. Feather was lost. If the letter had explained everything when Urania *had* written it (it was hard to be sure), what did it explain if she *hadn't?*

Mimi made herself heard above the din. "After the pie-flinging began," she explained, "Urania needed help. We all tried to do what we could. I wrote the letter, because I knew how to write it in a way Kokopelli couldn't resist. I lured him here with flattery!"

So. The letter didn't explain anything. Well, maybe there was nothing left to explain.

"Flattery?" said the imp, waving the letter. "What flattery? It says, 'witty, intelligent, lively, and cute . . . an irresistible gravitational force . . .' That isn't flattery. It's the plain truth!"

"And I helped Urania build her chadium umbrella and the multitipped laser wand," Chad chimed in, ignoring Kokopelli's outburst, "and Aeiou wrote all the software."

Kokopelli scowled, or sounded as if he were scowling. "You two! I always knew you weren't on my side."

"Science doesn't take sides," said Chad matter-of-factly. "It works on interesting problems. As I explained earlier, remote-controlled Smart Pies and pie defense both offer some fascinating challenges."

Kokopelli would have been red in the face had he not been a silhouette. "Betrayed by science," he muttered, then wheeled on Feather. "And how did *you* betray me, my feathered so-called friend?"

Feather racked his brain, trying to think of something. "Um . . . I waited outside Mimi's house once, when I could have gone inside?"

"Pathetic," sneered Kokopelli. "Some helper. And you two . . ." He turned on Pwt and Bo, who had no idea what anyone was talking about. "You didn't help her, but you didn't help me, either. Well, you should have! YOU SHOULD HAVE HELPED MEEE! Ha ha ha ha ha ha!"

The imp laughed maniacally for a long time. "Let me thank you all, my enemies, for gathering here together in one place. How perfect! Just where I want you, every one . . . because I've prepared a little surprise for you all—just in case the *talking* didn't work out."

"Wh-what is it?" Feather asked.

"A pie, of course, a big, beautiful, sticky pie, the Smartest Pie that ever was. You can't escape it now, none of you." He touched the button on Feather's chest. "Just look around you, pal."

Feather instinctively looked at the other Muses before he realized what he was doing. Now he had made targets of them all, including himself. (The chubby Muse of Plants had glimpsed his own bright orange beak in a small mirror over Chad's desk. Kokopelli, meanwhile, had slipped a bag over his own head and put up a sheet of paper in front of Emma's face to block the camera's view.) The situation, Feather reflected, could be serious. Who knew how big, or heavy, or full of lumps this Smartest Pie might be? And if it wiped them all out, how would he get any doughnuts? What could he do?

"Quick, Feather," said Emma. "Follow me! You, too, Aeiou!" In one hand she clasped Feather's big orange paw, in the other she took Aeiou's long sleeve, and she pulled both Muses out of the room. Crraw followed to act as interpreter. Feather's stubby legs churned, and his toes banged into stray cyclotron parts.

As they trotted out of the dome, Feather could hear

Kokopelli screaming with rage, followed by scuffling, some attempts at reasonable conversation, more screams, and some thumping. The noise faded into the distance. Emma led Feather, Aeiou, and Crraw into the Great Hall of the Pie Flinger. It was pitch dark. Feather heard rattling and slapping. Crraw's voice croaked, "Aeiou says where is it? Where's the light switch?"

Feather wondered how Crraw could interpret Aeiou in the dark.

"Ah, here we are!" said Crraw. A click, and the room was flooded with brilliant white light.

Before them loomed the vast apparatus of computers, generators, engines, sensors, pie ovens, pulleys, cables, and belts, and above it all the menacing, pie-flinging arm. At the top, its monstrous mitt clutched the most frightening pie ever baked: at least thirty feet across, three tons in weight, divided into eight segments, and bristling with spikes and lumps and some of the ugliest frozen strawberries Feather had ever seen. It twitched and hummed and gave every sign of preparing to spring to life.

"Aeiou says ingenious," muttered Crraw. "The pie can break apart into pieces that can hunt down the Muses one by one . . . and she asks, what do you want her to do?"

"Erase the targets!" cried Emma. "Deprogram it from aiming at Muses!"

As Aeiou tapped at a keyboard, Feather gazed up at the mighty machine. Its image flashed from his headdress

camera to receptors in the comput-
erized base. Aeiou typed in code
that erased all the pictures of
Muses. A new image—the image
of the pie flinger itself—sped
through electronic circuits to
the memory chips in the
Smartest Pie's guidance
system. Radio beacons
bounced off satellites.
The target's position
was calculated.

The great arm
began to creak. It slowly ratcheted back,
clicking notch by notch, straining against unseen
springs in the base. It whirred and swiveled this way
and that before locking into position with a surprising
squeak. Then it fired. The pie-paw swung forward, slowly
at first, then faster and faster until it blurred into a pinkish
flash high above their heads. The massive pie shot off
through a hole in the roof. It rose higher and higher until
it vanished into the night sky.

"Well, that's gone," said Feather. "Now what?"

Soon a distant speck of light appeared in the heavens. It grew larger. The pie seemed to be falling straight at
them. Below, in the lab, the machine set up its defenses.
Chadium umbrellas unfurled with a rustle and pop. Glassy

filaments like the ones on Urania's wand sprouted from slots in the machine. Beams of laser light shot into the sky and gradually merged into one brilliant ruby line aimed at the falling pie. The three Muses and one Human backed away from the machine.

The pie swerved. The beam missed its target. Rocket motors coughed into life, slowing the pie's descent. With a loud crack, it broke into eight wedges, each one flying under its own power. They swooped down toward the chadium shields, probing for weaknesses. The laser beams again split apart and swept the sky like searchlights, as the pie pieces dodged and weaved. One laser found its mark. A wedge exploded and fell to earth in a shower of crust, whipped cream, strawberries, and other lumps. A metallic shard sliced through a chadium umbrella, peeling it back like a banana skin.

The nearest surviving pie piece sensed the hole and hurtled toward it. A laser took it out with a gooey blast, but a third wedge followed right behind and shot through the gap. It crashed straight into the flinger arm, which buckled, snapped, and fell into the base with an awful sound of tearing metal and breaking glass.

The chadium shields began to sway. Some of the lasers winked out. The remaining pie pieces zigzagged around the defenses. Two umbrellas succeeded in stopping the attackers with a harmless *pof,* but the last three wedges found their mark and plowed into the machine.

Computer screens went blank. Severed wires fizzed and sparked. Several small fires broke out. Sticky, lumpy billows of strawberry cream settled into the machine, dousing the fires as they oozed into the works and seeped out the cracks.

"Chad is going to be *so* upset," Feather said at last, and added inwardly, I am *never* going to get my doughnuts.

Aeiou's right sleeve leaped to her forehead while her left whizzed around in a fair imitation of the ruined machine.

Crraw translated.

"Aeiou says not to worry. She and Chad understand the design perfectly. They can always build another one if they want to."

With that reassuring thought, they went to tell the others what had happened.

16

Urania's Failure

EVERYONE CHEERED WHEN Emma, Crraw, Aeiou, and Feather returned to the observatory—everyone except Kokopelli, of course. His mechanical pie-flinging days were finished. The Great Pie War was over. The Muse of Tricks stood stock-still, stunned, his arms dangling like ribbons. But when the other Muses crowded around the four and slapped their backs and shook their hands and offered their congratulations and thanks, Kokopelli came back to life.

"Emmaaaaaaaa!" he wailed. "How could you do this to me, Emma? Emmaahahahaaa! I thought you were my friend!"

"I am your friend, Kokopelli," said Emma.

"But look what you've done to my *project*," he sobbed. "I thought you were *helping* me!"

"Well, I was. Sometimes."

"But—"

"Let me explain," said Emma.

About time, thought Feather. He was still a little bit confused. He thought Emma was helping Kokopelli, too; except, that is, when she was helping Urania. But how could she help both of them, when they were at war? Maybe she was . . . was . . . was . . .

"From the beginning," Emma went on, "I've been trying to sort out my life with my foster father, Mr. Drinkwater."

That . . . oversized, virulent *Daktulosphaira vitifoliae,* Feather added inwardly.

"Ever since I saw that piece of paper in his wallet—the one that fitted the scrap I had in my dresser—I knew I had to understand the message we saw when he combined the two. I hoped—I still hope—that it will give me some important clue about my parents and let me find out more about myself and my family history."

Feather thought this sounded reasonable, though of course he could never be sure. Plants made so much more sense.

"Almost as soon as I arrived here in Kokonino County, I knew that Urania, Muse of Astronomy, was the one who could help me the most."

Feather sagged a bit. Hadn't he helped, too?

"Feather was nice, too. He was generous and warm. But he wasn't mathematical. He fed me and listened to my problem, and just as important, he took me to Urania."

Well, then, that was better.

"Unfortunately, Urania was too busy dodging pies to help me. I decided to protect her at all costs. When I learned about the mechanical pie flinger and Kokopelli's plans for it, I urged Chad to build some defenses against Kokopelli's pies. That's why Chad made the chadium umbrella that I gave to Urania before the first attack of Smart Pies."

Aeiou flapped her sleeves. "Aeiou says very logical," translated Crraw.

"You?" said Kokopelli. "You gave the umbrella? And didn't tell me?"

Emma shrugged and went on. "As I got to know Kokopelli, I realized he would never give up—"

"She *does* understand me, you have to admit," said Kokopelli, brightening slightly.

"Never give up," she went on, "until he either got his way and pied Urania, or was stopped completely. So I hung around him and learned all his plans; meanwhile, I also visited Chad alone and encouraged him to work just as hard on stopping Smart Pies as on aiming them. I even helped Kokopelli at times, because I wanted to speed the whole thing along to end it sooner. And besides, I liked being around him!"

"Well, of course you did. Who wouldn't?" purred the Muse of Tricks.

"There seemed to be two possibilities: either a pie so powerful it could destroy its own flinger, or else Kokopelli and Urania would make peace."

"Never for long!" chuckled the imp, and he began to play a tune on his flute.

"All the time pies were getting bigger, smarter, and more destructive," continued the girl, raising her voice, "Mimi and I discussed ways to bring Kokopelli and Urania together to talk. Mimi wrote a flattering letter to Kokopelli . . . really buttered him up . . . and as you all saw, he took the bait."

"Took the bait? I was totally ready for you! Every one of you would be pie goo right now, if only that stupid Feather hadn't—"

"Listened to me, instead of you?" concluded Emma with a triumphant smile. "I think even Feather is smart enough to know when to protect himself."

Feather glowed inwardly. She thought he was smart! But what did she mean, "even"?

"And now," said Emma, beaming with joy, "Urania is finally free of the pie threat, and she can concentrate on decoding the message from my parents!"

"I *do* feel much more *relaxed—*," Urania started to say, when Kokopelli's laughter interrupted her.

"Tricked!" he roared. "Me! The Muse of Tricks, tricked by you, a Human. Wow."

Kokopelli was never one to hold a grudge.

"I knew you were a champion trickster, Emma, but this is amazing. The master bows down to your greatness!" And he did, his snaky hairs brushing the floor. "If you need help, I won't stand in your way," he went on. "Please, Urania! Do whatever this girl wants!"

"Um . . . what about me?" put in Feather. "Do I get my doughnuts now?"

Kokopelli just cackled.

Urania's gaze drifted off into the distance, a clear sign of mental arithmetic. She began muttering. "QAZXRCGB97YR00WWBB," she said, "QAZXRCGB97YR00WWBB . . . QAZXRCGB97YR00WWBB . . . now, why isn't . . . ? What if . . . ? Should it be 'R00W' or 'ROOW'? Hm hm hm hm hmmmmmmmm."

Feather looked around. The other Muses were beginning to fidget, all except Bo, who stared stolidly off into space as any cow would do.

"Does anyone here have a paper and pencil?" Urania asked. Chad ducked out of the room for a moment and returned rolling a tall dolly loaded down with several large boxes. He ripped one open, pulled out a ream of letter-sized paper, and passed it to Urania, along with a box of pencils. She laid out a sheet of paper neatly. She sharpened a pencil. She scribbled madly. The first sheet was quickly covered with calculations, then a second, a third, fourth, fifth . . . until the Muse of Astronomy was surrounded by a blizzard of paper that settled at her feet like a snowdrift up to her waist. She had worn nine pencils to stubs. She frowned.

"Harder than I thought," she said. Several moans went up from the group. Feather noticed Emma chewing her cuticles.

Aeiou reached deep into one of her sleeves, pulled out a small computer bearing the Tiny Titan logo, and passed it to Urania, who scribbled quickly on its screen with a stylus. Everyone waited as the machine processed her instructions. And waited. And waited. All the while, Urania stared at its tiny display and frowned deeply.

A wisp of smoke emerged from the computer's side vent. The machine gave a flash and a wheeze, and the smoky wisp swelled into a great black cloud. The hand-held seemed to leap away from Urania. It hit the floor with a *crack*. Aeiou flapped her sleeves wildly.

"You fried the Tiny Titan!" screamed Crraw.

"I—I'm sorry," said Urania, holding her head in her hands. "I must have asked too much of its little circuits. I had no idea the problem was so hard."

"Wh-what d-do you mean?" asked Emma tremulously.

"I can't decipher the code. I've tried every formula known to Muse. Nothing works. I even blew out a computer, and the result is . . ." She held out her empty hands, palms up.

"NO-O-O!" shrieked Emma. "After all I've done! Saved you from . . . from . . . I don't know . . . death, probably . . . and . . . and . . . NOW YOU CAN'T DECODE THE SECRET MESSAGE?"

"No, I can't," said Urania. She closed her eyes, knitted her brows, and held the bridge of her nose between her right thumb and a long, tapering forefinger. "And now I have the most splitting headache. Math problems can be so *frustrating* sometimes."

Emma looked stunned. Her body began to tremble, which worried Feather, because when Kokopelli shook like that, it usually meant he was about to explode. But it turned out Emma was different from Kokopelli after all, and tears of disappointment began streaming down her cheeks like a flash flood gushing through a desert arroyo. The Muses crowded around to comfort her, but nothing seemed to help, not Chad's artificial prune juice, Feather's broccoli, or the soothing tunes from Kokopelli's flute.

"Ahem." The sound was loud and deep, as if it cleared an unusually big throat.

A low and gentle voice said, "The reason yooou couldn't decipher the mooo-ssage is that it isn't a mooo-ssage."

To find out who said this and what it meant, you will have to read the next chapter.

1 7

The Message

"IT'S NOT A CODED mooo-ssage."

Everyone turned around. Bo, the cow, was calmly chewing her cud and staring into space, as usual. She surveyed the crowd of Muses, until her large, luminous cow's eyes looked straight into Emma's.

"It's the pass code of a safe-deposit box."

Emma said nothing. She looked exhausted. Feather wondered if Chad had any refreshing green tea at the lab, but before he could ask, the cow continued.

"It's the pass code of safe-deposit box number QE-4B," Bo said, "in the Savings-R-Us Bank on Third Street."

"What's a safe-deposit box?" asked Emma listlessly.

Bo explained that many banks have a special vault

with locked metal boxes where customers can store especially valuable possessions. Each customer has a private pass code, something like an e-mail password, which ensures that only the owner can access the box.

"And how do you *know* it's the pass code of that particular safe-deposit box?" asked Emma.

Bo shrugged—no easy thing for a cow—and replied, "I don't know how I know. I just know. The same way I know that the Battle of Manzikert happened in 1071, or that Leonardo da Vinci wrote left-handed and backward, or that *Daktulosphaira vitifoliae* ruins grapevines, or—"

"You see, Emma," interrupted Feather, "Bo is the Muse of Factoids, or miscellaneous facts. She's not much for thinking, but her little cow-brain remembers the most amazing collection of odds and ends you could ever imagine. If she says it's a safe-deposit box pass code, you can believe her." What good this piece of information might be, Feather had no idea. He knew nothing about banks, except that the plants in their lobbies were usually artificial. He did, however, notice that several of the Muses were smiling.

"But this may be good news," said Emma, brightening a little. "The box's pass code came from my parents, so the box must have belonged to them! How does a person get into these safe-deposit boxes?"

"With a key."

"Wonderful!" She sighed. "I don't have the key. Where is it?"

"Good question!" Kokopelli cackled from behind the group. "Check *this* out!"

The crowd of Muses wheeled around. In the center of the room, high in the air, was a hovering image of an immense, blotchy ear. Beneath it, Kokopelli was twirling the dials of an Intelligent Air terminal. The view zoomed out to reveal the entire lumpy head. Everyone gasped. It was Drinkwater. At this size, his stubble poked up like fence posts on a cratered, discolored planet with a poisonous atmosphere. But, then, no one looks good in extreme closeup without makeup, not even movie stars. Several Muses averted their eyes.

"Kokopelli!" Urania hissed. "How long has he been listening?"

"Long enough, I imagine," chuckled Kokopelli, "to have heard everything."

Emma and the Muses watched in dismay as Drinkwater's little birdlike hand—at this magnification, about the size of a medium pizza—rose and began rubbing his stubble thoughtfully. His beady eyes, each one as large as a blue plum, narrowed to slits between his puffy eyelids as if crushed by a pair of enormous dumplings. A phlegmy rumble erupted from deep in the doughy man's throat.

"I wonder . . . ," he mused aloud. "What if it's the number of a *safe-deposit box?* That would explain what the old *key* was for . . . and I'll bet the box is at Savings-R-Us . . . just a hunch . . . but worth trying. . . ."

You could practically eat the dismay in Chad's observatory, thought Feather, it's that thick. And I'm that hungry. His stomach gave a bark that made Drinkwater jump.

"Shhhh!" whispered several other Muses.

They watched in horror as Drinkwater picked up a shovel and stomped out his back door. In the dark garden, illuminated only by a slender sliver of moon, he began to dig wildly. His shadowy form strained and twisted, alternately plunging and hoisting. He worked silently, aside from the *chuf* of the shovel's impact and the *vump* of earth hitting earth, and gradually sank from sight in the deepening hole. The *chuf* changed to *clang.* "Pay dirt," he whispered. They could hear him wrestling with the buried strongbox. Suddenly there was a loud grunt, and the safe flew over the rim of the pit and settled into a hillock of earth.

Drinkwater clambered out. His little feet scampered back into the house. A door slammed twice. He returned with a flashlight and a blanket. He looked around nervously. Apparently satisfied that no neighbors were spying on him, he knelt down, draped the blanket over himself and the safe, and turned on the flashlight under the canopy. Only the faintest aura of light came through. The Muses heard the safe's dial spin, then the *chunk* of a handle. The silhouette shifted. Drinkwater had apparently opened the door and was removing something from inside. "Yes," he said quietly. Then louder, "YES!" The door slammed shut. The flashlight winked out. Drinkwater shrugged off his covering, and leaving blanket, safe, and flashlight in a heap, he hurried back indoors.

Kokopelli flipped a switch on his terminal, and the image winked out.

"Kokopelli!" roared most of the Muses at once. "Now you've really done it!"

"Done what?" asked Kokopelli innocently.

"Given Drinkwater the information!" cried Urania. "And a head start! Don't you see? There's no time to waste!"

"Actually," said Bo, "there's plenty of time to waste. The bank won't open until ten o'clock tomorrow morning."

"Very good!" chuckled Kokopelli. "Bo, you're not as dumb as you look!"

"Thank you," said Bo.

"Since you're all so intelligent," Koko continued, "ask yourselves this: how was Emma supposed to get the key, when it was locked in a safe buried six feet under? I just dug it up with no effort at all!"

"True," said Bo.

"And it was fun, too, because I got to watch all your stupid faces!" He laughed wildly. "Don't you see? I have a plan! Leave everything to me!"

Now there, thought Feather, is an idea that makes me really uncomfortable.

"I should *never* have given him that key," murmured Emma.

"Wait a minute," said Mimi. "Aren't we forgetting something? What about Mrs. Krishnamurti?"

"Yes," agreed Feather. "Wasn't Mr. Drinkwater going to poison her?"

"WHAT?" chorused several voices.

Feather described his last Intelligent Air view of Emma's foster father and teacher.

"Well, then," said Mimi, "we've got to hurry! What are we waiting for? Let's go!"

"Ah-ah-AH! Not so fast!" cried Kokopelli. "You'll mess up *everything!* If the eight of you go running off helter-skelter, who knows what may happen? Actually, *I* know: disaster! Chaos! Ruin! You all stay put! Remember—I have a plan!"

Now all the Muses started talking at once. Everyone, it seemed, had an opinion, but no one knew what to do. Gradually, the conversational eruption faded to a rumble, then a murmur, then an occasional hiccup, then silence. At last, someone pointed out that Kokopelli, unlike anyone else, at least *had* a plan, and it was certainly easier to follow somebody else's plan, once it existed, than to try to invent one all your own, even when this "somebody else" was unreliable, untrustworthy, and often destructive.

Emma, who had listened silently to all this, now spoke up. "It's O.K. to wait," she said. "I know Mr.

Drinkwater. He has a temper, sure . . . and he's greedy, we've all seen that . . . but he isn't a killer. All that talk of poison was just that—talk. I'm sure Mrs. Krishnamurti will be fine for a few more hours."

At this, everyone relaxed somewhat.

Feather was suddenly aware of Kokopelli's arm around his shoulder. The Muse of Tricks leaned in close and whispered, "Feather, old chum, our little Human friend is about to leave Kokonino County. Shouldn't you—you know?"

Feather nodded. He did know.

"All right, then, I'm off!" bellowed Kokopelli to the throng, without, however, moving his mouth away from Feather's ear. "Emma! Meet me at the bank tomorrow morning at 10 A.M. sharp!"

And he was gone. How did he *do* that?

The time had come for the Muses to say good-bye to Emma.

First Pwt, Muse of Animals, who barely knew her and so had little to say, then Crraw and Aeiou, then Mimi, Chad, Urania, and finally Bo. Every Muse was sorry to see her go. Emma looked sad, too, but also excited at the adventure before her. She thanked them all for their help and apologized for destroying so much valuable equipment.

"But before I leave," she said, "there's one thing I'd like to know. How does Intelligent Air work?"

Chad looked at Feather. Feather nodded slightly. So Chad told her.

"It's a computer network," he began. "Aeiou and I developed it just before the Muses got together back in . . . in . . ." He looked to Aeiou for help. She shrugged. "Some time ago," he finished lamely.

"As everyone knows, the chips that run computers have been getting smaller and smaller over the years. But I was the first to build an entire computer smaller than a grain of dust. Almost totally invisible! From there it was a simple matter—"

Aeiou's sleeves snapped. "Ha!" translated Crraw.

"O.K.," admitted Chad. "It was a lot of work, but we finally succeeded in setting up a factory to manufacture tiny computers by the billions." He waved his arm vaguely toward the main building.

"Maybe you noticed that mist rising from the pipes behind the lab? That's a cloud of invisible computers rising into the air. Once aloft, they circulate around the world, floating on the breeze like pollen grains. They're everywhere on earth. You can see them sparkling in sunbeams. Thousands of them fly up your nose every time you draw a breath."

Emma inhaled sharply, then coughed.

"Don't worry," said Chad, "they're perfectly harmless. No worse than the dust you breathe every day without noticing. And the beautiful thing is, nobody does notice. Not a soul on earth, aside from the nine Muses, is aware of Intelligent Air. No one has ever noticed the difference between ordinary dust and *my* 'dust.' Strange, because as computer chips keep shrinking, somebody should have foreseen this.

"Tiny computers aren't really that surprising. Everyone knew they were coming. But the software that connects them is truly astounding—the work of a real genius: my esteemed friend and colleague, Aeiou. She programmed the computers into a gigantic, worldwide, wireless network. Every chip constantly 'talks' to its neighbors, so all together they form a planet-spanning, elec-tronic 'nervous system.' New computers are constantly rising into the air to join the network, while old ones settle out and collect under furniture and in corners."

"Is that why people call them dust *mice?*" asked Emma with a smile. Chad looked blank, but Aeiou let out a small peep that surprised everyone.

"Every IA computer," Chad continued, "has video and audio sensors and transmitters, and soon we hope to add smell. The only way to access the network is through one of these terminals," he held up one of the button-studded balls, "and the only terminals belong to the Muses. We, and we alone, have the power to see, hear, and project our voices anywhere in the world." Chad spread his arms wide, as if to encompass the whole earth, and smiled warmly. "And, of course, we only try to help."

Except maybe Kokopelli, thought Feather.

"But couldn't humans build a terminal if they knew about Intelligent Air?" asked Emma.

Chad looked uncomfortable. "We call that 'reverse engineering'—building a machine based on someone else's hardware and software. It's not impossible. Understanding how the chips work would be fairly easy, but without the software . . . well . . . Aeiou? What do you think?"

Aeiou made a looping motion around her head.

"Aeiou says it isn't a problem, because the network is secret," said Crraw.

"But now *I* know about it," objected Emma.

"But we know you won't tell anyone," said Chad and Crraw in unison.

"How do you know that?"

Chad just shrugged. "Feather," he said, "I think it's time for our guest to go. She faces a full day tomorrow." The other Muses murmured their agreement, and frankly, they rushed Emma out of the room. Feather took her elbow, someone threw open the door, and a someone else gave her a gentle but definite shove. They all waved brightly and slammed the door behind her. She probably would have been offended, thought Feather, if she weren't so excited.

It fell to Feather to accompany the Human back to the border of Kokonino County. As they left the observatory, the immense licorice-black sky began to fade, the sprinkled stars grew less distinct, and high above them a few pink-frosted crullers of cloud appeared to herald the approaching dawn. The desert, as usual, was utterly silent except for the crunch of their feet on the gravel path. The machine-oil odor of Chad's lab faded and gave way to the delicate scent of cactus flowers and mesquite.

Emma turned for a last look. In the distance, flanked by expanses of sand and jumbles of stone, Chad's lab glinted in the morning sun, which had just poked a brilliant sliver over the distant mountains. As usual, mist rose steadily from the pipes and chimneys behind the lab.

"Intelligent Air," murmured Emma.

"Oh, that reminds me," said Feather. "We have to stop by my place before I deliver you to the border. I have to . . . ah . . . pick something up."

"What do you have to get?" inquired Emma.

"Get? Oh yes . . . ah . . . er . . ." As usual, Feather had forgotten to plan ahead. "Breakfast!" he blurted out at last. "Get some breakfast! For both of us! Especially you! You don't want to start your Big Day on an empty stomach!"

Emma had to agree. She nodded enthusiastically, and when they reached Feather's hut, he set out a vegetarian feast of candied peas with oatmeal, fried salted tofu, and fruit salad. Emma must have been hungry, because she ate it all.

When she had finished the last mouthful, Feather handed her a steaming mug of tea, one of his most powerful and tasty brews, its list of ingredients a carefully guarded secret. Bladderwort, certainly. Ginseng, possibly. Sarsaparilla root, probably. And when all of these were well steeped in hot water, the Muse added a few aromatic pinches of dried herbs, roots, and flowers known only to himself. Emma drained the whole mug at once. You would have, too; it was that good.

"I hate to leave," said Emma, leaning back and looking fondly at Feather. "It's fun here."

"But you have to," said Feather firmly.

"Yes," she said. "I have to."

Feather coughed. "Before you go, there's something I have to tell you. The tea you just drank was a Forgetfulness Potion. It will erase everything about us Muses from your mind."

"What?" Emma looked frightened.

"Kokonino County and your time here will fade from your consciousness. The rest of your memory will remain. Don't worry. You'll be fine."

"But why?"

"The world of Humans has to remain ignorant of the Muses, our ways, our Intelligent Air. You know too much. We can't let you give us away."

"But, Feather, I can keep your secret! I could lie! I wouldn't mind!"

"We think it would be too hard on you. It will be easier simply to forget. You won't remember I said this, but we'll always look after you, dear Emma. Maybe you can take up gardening so you and I can keep in touch."

"H-how fast is it going to happen?" she stammered.

"It varies. A couple of hours or a couple of days. It's hard to say right now. We'll just have to see. But it always works."

Emma began to cry. "I'm going to miss you, Feather."

"No, you won't. You can't miss something you don't remember."

"But I miss you right now!" And she threw her spindly arms around the Muse of Plants and hugged him like a gnat hugging a hippo.

"Don't be silly," said Feather in some embarrass-
ment. "You can't miss somebody who's still here!" Or can you? He was already missing Emma.

He gently removed her arms from around his waist, and hand in hand they walked into the bright desert morning. Within minutes, the two had covered the ground to the hidden passage in the rock, and after many good-byes, they parted.

Emma quickly made her way to the mall, where her bicycle was still parked, ready to carry her back to town.

Feather hurried back to Chad's, where the group of Muses, minus only Kokopelli, was still gathered to watch the trickster's plan unfold.

18

A Little Mistake

THE OTHER MUSES greeted Feather nervously. "Did she drink the potion?" "Will it take effect fast enough?" "Will she give us away?" "Are you sure she didn't just pretend to drink it?"

Feather wondered how much harm it would do if the Muses were discovered. Some of them, he was sure, would love the attention. But secrecy was best. If the Muses were known, there would be no end of Humans begging for help, and it hardly seemed fair to give all your attention to the loudest complainers. Besides, when you work in secret, no one can blame you for your mistakes! This was better, wasn't it?

Feather assured the others that Emma really had drunk the Forgetfulness Potion, so they stopped worrying about themselves and started worrying about Emma. Mimi activated her Intelligent Air terminal and summoned up a view of Third Street directly in front of Savings-R-Us, where Emma was supposed to meet Kokopelli.

Neither one of them seemed to be there.

Where was she? The Muses nervously conferred among themselves. Try the mall, one suggested. Her school, said another. Home, said a third. But why would she go home, when home was so dangerous? Try it anyway, just to be safe. Mimi spun the dial, and to everyone's surprise and dismay, Emma came into focus just as she was bounding up the steps to Drinkwater's front door.

Urania zoomed in to Emma's ear. "Don't do it!" cried seven Muses at once.

"Be quiet!" said Emma. "You can't stop me!" Here, thought Feather, was a perfect example of why Humans shouldn't know about Muses. Knowing where the voice in your head was coming from made it so much easier to ignore. Feather hoped the Forgetfulness Potion would take effect soon.

Just as Emma reached for the knob, the door swung open. There stood Darien Drinkwater. He was unusually well-dressed today. His blimplike body had been squeezed into a nice toast-colored suit, and his clean-shaven face gleamed as if polished. He was holding a suitcase.

Drinkwater scowled down at Emma. "You," he said simply. "You had to come back." He sounded almost sad.

Emma kicked his shin, but her foot bounced off his fleshy body, and he only smiled. "I know what you've done!" she shouted. "And you won't get away with it!"

"Oh, dear," muttered Mimi. "I wish she'd calm down."

Drinkwater's face, already pale, went utterly white. His lips moved silently like a pair of albino fish. At last he choked out a few words. "You . . . know . . . what . . . I've . . . done . . . ?"

"Yes! And—"

Before she could say another word, her foster father lurched forward, encircled Emma's waist with one thick, flabby arm, clamped his other hand over her mouth, picked her up bodily, and whisked her into the house. The door slammed shut. Furious, muffled screams emerged through the big man's puffy little paw. He dragged the girl toward the basement stairs, muttering to himself, "Knows what I've done, knows what I've done, knows what I've done . . ." He kicked open the door—which no longer seemed to be locked—and dragged her downstairs. She struggled and writhed, but in vain.

In the dim light of the basement, little had changed. The filing cabinet still lay on its side, although it had been pushed back against the wall and out of the way. The loosened window bar had been replaced and cemented in with a fresh gob of mortar. The pile of sandwich leavings, which still lay on the table, had grown fuzzy with greenish gray mold. Emma peered into the darkness.

"Wh-what's that?" she said at last when her eyes had adjusted. She pointed at a long bundle lying stiffly on the couch. Something was wrapped in a blanket and tied round and round with the paper ropes woven by Mrs. Krishnamurti.

"That? That was your teacher."

"WAS? What do you mean?"

"Dead," said Drinkwater simply. "Dead. I thought you said you knew what I'd done."

"Oh no," wailed Mimi softly. "We've failed her." If only, recalled Feather guiltily, he had told her about the edible mushrooms . . .

"Yes, my sweet, I poisoned her," said Drinkwater half hysterically. "And you're next, I'm afraid! I really hate to do it, but you know too much!"

The big man began pacing the floor in his small polished shoes, while Emma sat by the bundle on the sofa and glared at him.

"The victim here," he said wildly, "is me. I told her again and again how sorry I was. I never wanted to hurt anyone . . . but things happened. I've made mistakes, I know that, but everyone makes mistakes, and haven't I tried to make it up to you? But somehow everything went wrong . . . and you didn't make it any easier, with your tricks, your disruptions, and your disappearance! If you hadn't left school, she'd have never—"

"What are you talking about, make it up to *me?*" asked Emma. Apparently she still had her wits about her.

Drinkwater stopped pacing. He seemed to be debating with himself. He looked at one hand, and then at the other. At last he spoke.

"Why do you think I took care of you all those years? Because I liked all the bother and expense? No! I never wanted a brat around the house! But I did it to make things right with you!"

"Would you quit talking in riddles?" asked Emma heatedly.

"It all started a long time ago," said Drinkwater, "one day when I was out driving with my wife. We were having an argument. I may have lost my temper just a little bit. If you must know the truth, I was half yelling. To be perfectly honest, I was screaming at the top of my lungs with my eyes closed. Such a little mistake. But that's the reason I didn't notice the car stopped at the red light directly in front of us. A green Ford, it was."

Emma's eyes widened in horror. "Our car was a green Ford," she murmured.

"Yes . . . we plowed into its rear end at full speed," he said, almost dreamily, as if reliving it all in slow motion. "The Ford shot forward into the intersection and all the cross traffic. A brick truck coming from the left took out the whole front end. Smashed it flat as a pancake." He smacked his little hands together.

"You!" shrieked Emma. "You were the hit-and-run driver! You're the one who—"

"No, no, NO! It wasn't my fault! I just took my eyes off the road for a second! And then BANG! BANG!" He slapped his hands together twice. "Amazingly enough, I wasn't injured, and my car would still go. Without thinking, I steered around the wreckage and drove off as fast as I could. Luckily for me, I owned a building just around the corner—the big warehouse at Minus One Sixth Street. I was able to drive my car into the freight elevator and take it down to the basement, where I hid it behind a few pallet loads of refrigerators. The police never suspected me, and I've been free to this day."

"Monster," growled Emma.

"Not at all," moaned Drinkwater, his eyes welling up with tears of self-pity. "I just made a little mistake. I'm really a good person." He sniffed. "I couldn't turn myself in, you see, because I had to take care of my wife. She suffered a head injury that made her lose all memory of the accident. It was awful. I swore to myself that I would never be angry again. I would be sweet and kind and patient. And I vowed to make it up to you, too. As soon as my wife recovered, we took you in. And for several years, wasn't I the sweetest man that ever lived?"

Emma said nothing.

"You don't believe me?" Drinkwater continued. "Then think of this: I only took *half* your precious message from your parents, and I kept your key safely locked up.

You see? Isn't that nice? I could have taken *everything!* I could have done whatever I *wanted!*"

Emma muttered something under her breath that was hard to catch, but it sounded unpleasant.

"Yes, I was sweet," Drinkwater whined, "but I suffered. Oh, how I suffered! Well, not anymore! I'm taking whatever's in your safe-deposit box and I'm leaving for Paraguay, before they discover—" And he waved at the shrouded body of Mrs. Krishnamurti.

"You'll never get away with it."

Drinkwater looked thoughtful. "I'm sorry you came back, Emma. If you'd stayed away, I could have left in peace, and I wouldn't have to poison you. But now you really leave me no choice."

He began uncorking a number of purple-and-green bottles that stood on the table next to the decaying sandwiches. He poured some sinister-looking syrup into a dirty glass, then added a pinch of pale pink powder. The syrup began to foam wildly.

"I won't drink it," said Emma.

"Oh, I think you will," he said firmly and stepped toward her with the evil-looking liquid, which jumped around in the glass and changed colors.

"NO-O-O!" shouted all the Muses at once.

At the sound, Drinkwater set down the glass. He put his hands to his head. "Aghh! Those voices again!" he screamed.

"STOP! STOP! STOP! STOP!" shouted the Muses.

The big man in his tight suit began leaping around the small confines of the basement. Emma cowered behind the filing cabinet to avoid being trampled. "GO AWAY! SHUT UP! LEAVE ME ALONE!" he bellowed.

"WE WON'T! WE WON'T! WE WON'T! WE WON'T!" yelled the Muses.

With a crazed look in his eye, Drinkwater charged toward the stairs. "I'll deal with you later, you . . . you . . . cockroach! On my way to the airport! Right now I gotta get outta here!" He ran up the stairs and out the door, locking it behind him. The Muses could hear the sound of feet treading on the floorboards above. A door slammed. The house fell silent.

"Well, Muses, a fine mess you've made," said Emma angrily to no one in particular. "Save your suggestions, please. You tried to help Mrs. Krishnamurti, and now she's . . ." Her voice trailed off. "Well," she shouted, "doesn't anyone have anything to say?"

Nobody did.

"Well, fine! I'm used to being on my own! If the Muses can't help me, maybe a human being can. Help!" She yelled at the top of her lungs. "HELP! HELP!" She shouted until her strength gave out, and then she sat silently and rested.

The Muses began debating among themselves. What should they do first, save Emma or stop her former foster father? With regret, Mimi picked up her Intelligent Air terminal, spun the dial, and the Muses took one last look at the small, sad girl, alone in the dark basement with its jumbled furniture and the still form of Mrs. Krishnamurti lying bundled in a blanket on the dusty sofa.

1 9

D r . M o m o h

MIMI'S TERMINAL SUMMONED up a wide view of Third Street with Savings-R-Us in the middle of the block, between a Starbucks and a Krusty-Glop shop, the sight of which made Feather moan softly. Kokopelli was nowhere in sight. The Intelligent Air view wandered down the block and turned the corner onto Slowe Lane. Soon Drinkwater's hulky, bulky form lurched into view. His shiny head gleamed visibly from a long way off. He was frowning deeply.

At the corner, where people were waiting for the light to change, Drinkwater suddenly looked sharply to his left. Because of the crowd, it was hard to see what had drawn his attention. Something or someone seemed to be tugging at his sleeve, because the disgruntled giant was frowning at his own elbow. The light changed. The crowd moved on.

Only two people remained standing at the curb: Darien Drinkwater and, by his side, a very short man in a broad-brimmed hat and a cheap suit. Mimi zoomed in for a better look.

The little man's hat brim dipped so low that it shielded his face from view. His suit was cut from a tasteless plaid of red, orange, and electric blue. He slouched and darted furtive glances in all directions. Nothing about him inspired trust—until, that is, he started to speak. His voice was astonishingly warm, friendly, persuasive, melodious. It was a voice no one could resist, the kind of voice that draws people to follow it into grand schemes, wild projects, and yes, foolish mistakes, just because they want to hear more of it.

"Excuse me," said the fascinating voice, "aren't you Darien Drinkwater?"

"Nnngh?" Drinkwater stared at the short man as if hypnotized.

"I thought so," said the man sweetly. "Please allow me to introduce myself. I am Dr. Eze Momoh of the Nigerian Development Bank. I am happy to make your acquaintance." He extended his hand. In a daze, Drinkwater took it and allowed his own hand to be shaken vigorously.

"My people at the bank," continued Dr. Momoh, "have asked me to approach you with an opportunity that is very confidential and totally top secret. We need your help in transferring *a huge sum of money* in the strictest confidence. May I tell you my story?" He made the question sound like an invitation to a picnic beside a babbling brook on a beautiful spring day.

"Nnh-hh," breathed Drinkwater uncertainly.

"A certain foreign gentleman, a Dr. Edmund Maples, who invested heavily in oil wells in my native Nigeria, recently met his death in the unfortunate crash of the ill-fated Kenya National Airlines flight KQ431. Perhaps you know of it? No? It occurred last January 20, on a Sunday. No one survived."

"Last January 20 wasn't a Sunday," whispered Urania before the other Muses could shush her.

"The Nigerian Development Bank, where I work," resumed Dr. Momoh, "has a balance of *thirty-two million American dollars* on deposit belonging to Dr. Maples. Since he has died, we would like to move this money out of our country."

The mention of thirty-two million dollars seemed to focus Drinkwater's attention somewhat.

"We are looking for a trustworthy partner," said the loud-suited man with the soft voice, "with an American bank account. Someone like yourself, Mr.

Drinkwater. We would like to transfer the *thirty-two million dollars* into your account temporarily before moving most of it out to pay the poor, deserving heirs of Dr. Maples what they are due. You would retain 15 percent of the total amount, to keep for yourself, as payment for your help."

"Fifteen percent?" said Drinkwater. "That would be . . . ah . . . ahhhhhh . . ."

"Four point eight million American dollars exactly. At absolutely no risk to yourself, I might add."

"Whoa!" said Drinkwater. "Let me think about this."

"Yes, by all means, think," said Dr. Momoh, "but please don't think too long. I have a list of several other people besides yourself who would make trustworthy partners. I'd hate for you to lose the *four point eight million dollars,* but if you'd rather I gave the opportunity to someone else . . ."

"No, no! Wait!" protested the pasty behemoth. "Wait! Don't go! Just one second. Tell me . . . supposing I were to go for this . . . scheme, what exactly would I have to do?"

"First, Mr. Drinkwater, our bank would require some proof of your honesty and trustworthiness. We must have absolute confidence in you, Mr. Drinkwater; surely you can appreciate that, when *thirty-two million dollars* are at stake."

"Yes, yes, of course."

"I will need to keep some token of yours, some trifling

personal possession, nothing important really, and only until the funds have arrived, at which time I shall return it to you. You won't even miss this little item, everything will happen so quickly. As you know, Mr. Drinkwater, money moves electronically now, and the *thirty-two million dollars* will be wired from Nigeria to your American bank in a matter of minutes. It could be here by eleven o'clock this morning."

Drinkwater licked his lips. That voice! It made the phrase "thirty-two million dollars" sound like all the wonderful things of the world: a doughnut, a day at the beach, a week in Paris, the smell of fresh-cut grass. In fact, Feather reflected, a person could exchange that much money for a lot of those things, and still have enough left over to retire in some tropical paradise.

"O.K., I'm your man," agreed Drinkwater.

"Wonderful!" Dr. Momoh sounded boundlessly happy. "Wonderful. So you won't mind lending me your wallet and house keys for the next forty-five minutes?"

"Forty-five minutes? Not at all." Emma's foster father produced the items in question from his pockets and handed them over.

"Now," said the African banker, "if you'll just wait for me over there," he indicated a massive stone building across the street, "I'll run my errand and quickly return with your things."

"Over *there?*" Drinkwater blanched. The building was the city's main police headquarters.

"Yes!" chortled Momoh persuasively. "Don't you see? This is how I prove *my* trustworthiness to *you!* I would never agree to meet you *there* if I were involved in anything that was less than 100 percent legal and honest, now would I?"

"I see your point, Dr. Momoh. Or may I call you Eze?"

"Call me anything you like, my friend, just don't call me late for our date with *thirty-two million dollars!*"

With that, the golden-voiced midget sped around the corner, while Drinkwater, his heart pounding in anticipation of endless tropical drinks with little umbrellas in them on a beach in the South Seas, took a seat on a sticky bench in front of a building full of police.

20

The Vault

INSTEAD OF STOPPING at Savings-R-Us, the African banker hurried past it, turned the next corner, and doubled back in the direction from which he had come.

"Follow that man!" whispered several Muses, and the Muse of Getting Along with People obeyed. Unlike Mr. Drinkwater, who was tall and had a shiny head, the short Dr. Momoh often vanished into the crowd, but Mimi caught enough glimpses of his wild plaid to follow him all the way to Drinkwater's house. Here, using Drinkwater's keys, he let himself in. Without hesitation, he went straight to the basement door.

"He certainly seems to know what he's doing," Feather whispered.

Momoh unlocked the door and went down.

Emma still sat as they had left her, listlessly waiting for whatever came next. When she saw the little man come down the stairs, she trembled in fear, and no wonder. He certainly looked bizarre. Then he spoke.

"Emma!" he said in his musical voice. "Kokopelli sent me!"

"Who?" she said nervously.

"Never mind," said the man. "Let's just say I'm a friend."

"Prove it," said Emma tartly. The charms of Momoh's speech seemed not to affect her.

Dr. Momoh reached into his pocket and pulled out Drinkwater's wallet and keys. From the wallet he produced a faded slip of paper.

"Here," he said, "is the pass code of your parents' safe-deposit box, and here," holding up the key ring, "is the key. You, I believe, have your own fingerprints. Perhaps you'd like to bring them to the bank to identify yourself? Would you like to open your box now?"

Emma looked startled. "But . . . look! Mrs. Krishnamurti has been murdered! Shouldn't we go straight to the police?"

"Sweet child, don't worry about any of that," said the African in his most reassuring voice, which was very reassuring indeed.

The bundle on the sofa sat up. Emma screamed.

Muffled grunts came from under the blanket. The wrapped form wrestled and struggled against the ropes

wound around it. Dr. Momoh rushed to the sofa and, after a bit of confusion, he and Emma untied everything. The blanket fell away to reveal the wan face of Mrs. Krishnamurti, looking tired and queasy, but very much alive.

"Ugh," said Mrs. Krishnamurti. "What was that awful stuff I drank? It must have contained beef broth."

Dr. Momoh pointed at a side table, where a glass still held the liquid intended for Emma. He picked it up and sniffed. "Hmm. Garlic powder and apricot syrup," chuckled the African. "Gross!" Beside the glass, a book was spread open, facedown. The title, which the Muses could see clearly, was *Poisons and Other Parlor Tricks for the Practical Prankster.* The author's name claimed to be I. M. Nutz.

Emma turned the book over and looked at the open page. It was a recipe for "Sickening Juice," and although it listed some fairly disgusting ingredients, there was nothing harmful or dangerous about it. And no meat products, to Mrs. Krishnamurti's relief.

"Hahaha!" said Dr. Momoh merrily. "Your foster father seems to have made a poor choice of murder weapons. He must have pulled the first book off the shelf that said 'poison.' Or maybe someone *suggested* it to him, who knows? Hahaha! People should really pay better attention to what they are doing. Poor Mrs. Krishnamurti was so exhausted from her struggles and lack of food that she passed out when she drank it. How are you feeling, Mrs. Krishnamurti?"

"Fine, I think. My foot hurts. The filing cabinet fell on it, but I doubt it's anything worse than a bruise. I feel hungry and very weak."

The African pulled a packet from his pocket. "Would you like a cup of miso soup with tofu and sea vegetables?" he asked. "Is there a microwave oven upstairs, Emma?"

Both replied yes. The little man bounded up the stairs two at a time. Kitchen sounds echoed down the stairwell while Emma filled in her teacher about Darien Drinkwater. Within five minutes, Dr. Momoh returned with a steaming bowl of soup, which Emma's teacher gratefully and greedily swallowed. Lovely vegetables, thought Feather happily. They'll bring back her strength in no time. And indeed, as soon as she had finished, Mrs. Krishnamurti stood up and began pacing around the room.

"There's work to be done," she said. "That awful man mustn't be allowed to walk the streets a minute longer. For all we know, he may be on his way to the airport right now. Or worse: he may be preparing another horrible crime. We have to get moving and stop him, Mr.—er, what did you say your name is?"

"I didn't. I am Dr. Eze Momoh, of the Nigerian

Development Bank, and I am pleased to make your acquaintance. But please, I beg you, don't be hasty. Before bothering ourselves about a sweaty, incompetent oaf who can't even pick out a proper book of poisons, there is another matter of the utmost importance that we need to attend to. I wonder if you would care to join us. I'm sure it would make Emma feel more comfortable to have an old friend by her side."

The teacher hesitated. "I don't know. Emma, what do you think?"

Emma answered immediately. "For some reason— I wish I knew why—I trust Dr. Momoh. Let's do as he asks."

A few minutes later, they entered the Savings-R-Us Bank—having come by a roundabout route to avoid walking past the police station on Slowe Lane. They stopped just inside the door. "Wait here," said Momoh. "Let me do the talking."

Eight Muses watched, along with Emma and Mrs. Krishnamurti, as Dr. Momoh approached the bank manager, a cheerful, chubby woman with purplish hennaed hair and pink-rimmed winged glasses hanging on a chain around her neck. The little man easily struck up a conversation, in which Feather heard words like *intestate* and *sole surviving heir* and *identification,* words that meant nothing to a Muse of Plants.

The two spoke for some time. Eventually, the musical voice won over the manager, who nodded her agreement to everything. She left her desk and returned shortly with a rather shabby-looking ledger book under her arm. Dr. Momoh waved to Emma. She approached. The manager asked if she was indeed Emma Sanderson. Emma said she went by Emma Drinkwater, and the manager said that was fine, her friend had explained everything. Would she mind giving a fingerprint sample?

The woman opened the book and laid a small ink pad on the desk before Emma. Taking Emma's hand gently in her own, the manager rolled the little fingers one by one across the pad and pressed them onto one of the book's large pages, just below another set of prints labeled "Sanderson." The new prints were larger than the old ones, but even Feather could tell they were a perfect match.

"And would you please write down your pass code?" asked the manager, handing Emma a piece of paper.

Emma carefully printed, "QAZXRCGB97YR00WWBB."

"Very good, Miss Sanderson," said the manager. "Come this way."

"May I bring my friends with me, please?"

"If you like."

The manager led the three visitors to the rear of the bank, where a small staircase led down to the basement. "What? Another basement?" groaned Feather. "Shh," hissed four or five other Muses. They descended into a brightly lit room with a green shelf along the wall on their right. At intervals a number of pens were tethered to fixtures by small chains, as if leashed to keep them from running away. Several small pads of paper kept them company. The rear wall of the room was entirely taken up by an enormous door, which, as it stood slightly open, they could see was at least a foot thick.

At a slight tug from the manager, the thick door swung open smoothly and silently. She unlocked a barred inner door, opened it, and ushered the three into the vault. The walls around them were a great grid of little metal doors, each door with two keyholes.

"Do you have your key?" asked the manager. Dr. Momoh fumbled noisily with Drinkwater's set until he found the one he wanted, a stubby steel key, which he

raised high, letting the others fall and jangle below on their ring. The manager consulted her ledger book.

"QE-4B . . . QE-4B . . . ," she said, running her finger along an endless row of doors at Emma's eye level. At last she stopped at box QE-4B. The manager inserted her own key into one of the keyholes, gave it a quarter turn, and stepped politely back to the far corner of the room. Dr. Momoh put his key in the other slot, turned it, and opened the small door. He reached into the cubbyhole behind it and drew out a long metal box.

"Heavy," he said.

Stooping slightly, he lugged the container to the outer room and dropped it onto the shelf with a loud *clunk*. Emma tried to open it, but her hands were shaking too badly to clasp the latch. Her breath came fast and shallow. She could barely speak. She waved her hand at Dr. Momoh, who obligingly popped open the lid and swung it back. He stood on tiptoe (the shelf was rather high for him) and leaned over for a look.

"I hope you won't be disappointed," he said. "It seems to be mostly paper."

Inside the box, a large Manila envelope lay like a paperweight on top of a messy stack of ordinary writing paper. With trembling hands, Emma removed the envelope; carelessly, she held it open end down. A cascade of old photographs spilled onto the counter. Some depicted a baby, with and without its parents. Others showed a small child. Still others displayed a handsome adult couple, the man tall and fair-haired, the woman rather darker, her face ringed with a messy mass of curls. They were at home; they were on a camping trip; he posed with a new car; she stood smiling on a beach. On the back of each picture was a brief description written neatly in black ink: "Emma, six weeks," "Emma's fourth birthday party," "Kokonino vacation," and the like.

"Kokonino vacation?" said Emma, sounding confused. "But that's not possible!"

"Why not?" asked Dr. Momoh.

"Well, because . . . I don't know. I don't remember now, but for some reason, it can't be."

The potion was taking effect, thought Feather with satisfaction.

Someone had written on the envelope, "Even if you lose everything else, you can still keep your memories."

Emma burst into tears. "My parents!" she wailed. Mrs. Krishnamurti laid a comforting hand on her shoulder.

The bank manager anxiously approached from across the room. "Is everything all right?" she asked.

"Y-y-y-yes," Emma managed to stammer. "It's just that I'm so happy and sad at the same time, I can hardly b-bear it."

"What else is in there?" asked Dr. Momoh. His voice sounded unusually musical.

Mrs. Krishnamurti offered Emma a handkerchief. "Dry your eyes, dear," she said. "You don't want to drip on the paperwork." While the loud-suited African (who was still wearing his hat, Feather noticed) gathered up the photos and replaced them in their envelope, Emma dabbed her eyes and studied the box. A smaller envelope had been hiding beneath the large one. This, too, was unsealed. From inside, Emma pulled a single sheet of paper.

It read, "In case anything should happen to us, please contact my nearest living relative about making arrangements to take care of Emma. Write my cousin, Miss Sita Lal, 1520 Imperial Road, Bangalore, India."

Mrs. Krishnamurti gasped. She gripped the shelf tightly as if to stop herself from collapsing.

"Is everything still all right?" asked the bank manager.

"Yes, yes," she whispered. "Just let me regain my composure only. Emma, what was your mother's maiden name?"

"Hmm . . . ," said Emma thoughtfully. "I can't remember."

"It wasn't van Dusenberg, by any chance?"

"Yes! Now I remember! That was it."

Mrs. Krishnamurti threw her arms around Emma. "Dearest, I am your cousin!"

"What?!" said seven or eight voices at once.

"Yes," she explained. "Your mother's aunt, on a trip to India long ago, met an Indian, and they fell in love and got married. His family name was Lal. Those are my parents—my maiden name is Sita Lal—so your mother is my first cousin. You and I are first cousins once removed. I often heard about my American cousin, and although we used to write to each other, we never met. We both got married at about the same time (Krishnamurti is my married name), and after that we wrote less often—married life can be busy, and the time flies so—and eventually your mother's letters stopped coming entirely. I had no idea of her awful tragedy. When I came to the States, I tried to look her up, but without success. Well, now I seem to have found her."

And she burst into tears, too. "A curious natural mechanism, crying," said Chad sagely under his breath. "I wonder why Humans do it." "Shh!" said the others.

When she had recovered somewhat, Mrs. Krishnamurti asked, "Emma, would you like to come live with me?"

"Yes, Mrs. Krishnamurti," Emma replied. She clung to the older woman, who patted her curly head and stroked her cheek gently.

"AHEM!" Dr. Momoh cleared his throat with a bark. "What *else* is in the box?"

Emma unwound herself from the hug and peered in. The bottom of the box was covered with a thick layer of paper. The sheets seemed to have been stuffed in randomly

and then deliberately spread around to fill the box from edge to edge and front to back. Emma began removing the pages one by one.

"Why, they're all blank!" she exclaimed in bewilderment. "What's the point of this?"

"Keep digging," said Momoh. "That box was awfully heavy."

Emma kept pulling out paper—all blank—until at last she could feel something underneath. She pulled the final sheets aside.

The box was filled to half its height with bars of solid gold.

"Go ahead, touch it," said Dr. Momoh, smiling. "It looks as if there's enough to support you for a good many years to come."

Emma carefully lifted one of the bars, turning it over in her hand and hefting its surprising weight.

"It's all yours, Emma—isn't it?" Momoh asked the bank manager.

"Yes," she said. "The box was owned jointly by Emma *and* her parents. There will be no need for court proceedings. She can walk out of here with the gold today if she likes. Or, of course, you may leave it here for safe-keeping."

Emma was speechless.

"Oh, look," said the musical midget. "There's one more thing."

A small packet, made of a piece of paper folded over many times, lay nestled among the glowing yellow ingots. Emma unwrapped it. Out slithered a little gold chain attached to a golden pendant. The jewelry was in the form of a small humanlike figure, cut out flat in silhouette. From its head sprouted several spiky strands of hair. From its mouth emerged a flute, over which the body was bent as if the musician were putting his whole spirit into the tune.

"Kokopelli!" she said. Emma's face brightened into a broad smile. She looked happier than Feather had ever seen her. Suddenly a strange expression clouded her features, as if a surprising memory had passed through her mind, but it quickly faded and the smile returned.

"This makes me so happy!" she exclaimed. "And I can't even say why!"

"That's perfectly all right," said Dr. Momoh, and coming toward her, he took the pendant and hung it around her neck.

"Well," continued the little man, "things seem to be very much under control here. I believe my work with you is done—at least for now!"

With that, he turned on his heel and left the room before anyone had a chance to thank him or say good-bye. Mrs. Krishnamurti dashed up the stairs after him, but soon returned to say that Dr. Momoh was gone.

No Muse can tell the future, said Feather to himself, but it's fair to say that all of us expect Emma and Mrs. Krishnamurti to have a happy one. Emma has a friend to take care of her, plenty of money, and her family photos. Mrs. Krishnamurti has rescued her pupil, who also happened to be her cousin, from that . . . that . . . plant-destroying

Pomacea canaliculata Darien Drinkwater. Emma and her teacher smiled at each other as they packed the pictures and papers back into the box, and there the Muses left them as Mimi spun the dial on her Intelligent Air terminal to find out what would happen to Mr. Drinkwater.

2 1

Anger Management

DRINKWATER STILL SAT on his bench in front of the police station. His head was thrown back, and his mouth was open, because he had fallen asleep. Thunderous snores rattled his palate. Several puzzled police officers stood around him scratching their heads and wrinkling their noses, their queasy expressions suggesting that Drinkwater's breathing was not only loud, it was fragrant.

"Officers! Arrest that man!"

It was Dr. Eze Momoh. He had just come from the bank.

The police looked around in confusion. Momoh was shorter than most of the people they were used to, so they all looked over his head. Eventually, they lowered their sights and saw the accuser.

"Why?" asked one of them, whose badge identified him as Sergeant Keystone.

"Kidnapping. Attempted murder. Assault. Vehicular manslaughter. Fraud. You'll find all the evidence you need at his home," Dr. Momoh gave them the address, "and his warehouse," he gave another address, "and two reliable witnesses just around the corner in the safe-deposit room at the Savings-R-Us Bank."

Sergeant Keystone said to one of his officers, "Step round to the bank and see about this. Say, you," he said to Drinkwater, jostling his elbow, "you'd better wake up."

Drinkwater's beady eyes half opened. His head jerked forward. He looked confused by the platoon of police officers, but when he saw the African, he seemed to come to his senses.

"You," he growled. "You have my money?"

Dr. Momoh tossed Drinkwater his wallet. "Here you go," he said cheerfully. "And here are your keys. Thanks for the loan!"

"No, I mean my *four point eight million dollars*," said Drinkwater as he checked his wallet.

"I don't have the slightest idea what you're talking about."

"AAAARGHHH!" bellowed the other and, rather rashly considering how many police were around, lunged at the little man in the loud suit. Momoh dodged. Six police officers jumped Mr. Drinkwater and pinned him to the ground. It took all their strength to hold him down.

"Don't be too hard on him," said Dr. Momoh. "At times, he's surprisingly gentle."

At this point, the officer returned from the bank to say that he had found the two witnesses, who had confirmed everything the little man had said. They would come to the station in a few minutes to give their statements.

"You're under arrest," said the sergeant.

"I'LL GET YOU FOR THIS, MOMOH!" roared Drinkwater over his shoulder as six officers dragged him away.

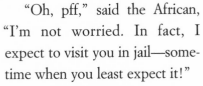

"Oh, pff," said the African, "I'm not worried. In fact, I expect to visit you in jail—sometime when you least expect it!"

"RAAARGH!"

"And don't forget to enroll in the anger-management classes! They can be very helpful!"

The roaring giant disappeared through the front door of police headquarters, and Dr. Momoh walked away humming to himself.

"I don't get it," said Feather to anyone who would listen. "What about the *thirty-two million dollars?* The Nigerian bank? The heirs of Dr. Maples?"

Dr. Momoh glanced furtively up and down the street to make sure no one was looking at him. He pulled a long stick from inside his plaid jacket—no, not a stick, a flute—raised it to his lips, and played a plaintive little tune. His jacket and hat shimmered and sparkled. Soon they seemed to dissolve completely, revealing a familiar, spiky-haired, silhouetted form.

"Kokopelli!" said Feather.

"There was no *thirty-two million dollars,* you idiot!" said the Muse of Tricks. "That was just a story to make the big oaf give up his wallet and keys."

He blew another tune on his flute. The jacket and hat reappeared, and "Dr. Eze Momoh" strolled away down the block.

How did he *do* that?

2 2

A Happy Ending

WHEN KOKOPELLI RETURNED to the observatory an hour later, all the Muses rushed to greet and congratulate him— all, that is, but one. Feather hung back in a sulk. Of course he was happy for Emma (though still disturbed about her garden), but why, he wondered, weren't the Muses cheering for *him*? If he hadn't destroyed the pie flinger almost single-handedly, Bo would never have told them about the safe-deposit box, and Kokopelli would still be heaving pies at Urania. Where would any of them be without the Muse of Plants?

He thought of all the time he had spent doing the trickster's bidding, and what did he have to show for it? It was worse than nothing. The other Muses were singing Kokopelli's praises, even though the devious little weasel had just spent two weeks trying to obliterate the Muse of Astronomy and swindle the Muse of Plants. WHERE ARE MY DOUGHNUTS? Feather wondered, and his stomach howled like a thousand wolves at a thousand moons. The more he thought about it, the gloomier he felt.

A sudden thought flashed through his mind. As thoughts sometimes do, this one seemed to pop up randomly, from nowhere in particular, and for no good reason at all. He found himself thinking back to Astronomy Night the evening before, not long after Kokopelli had arrived. Why, Feather wondered, did Kokopelli suddenly agree to talk? Why, when he saw all the Muses gathered together, hadn't the trickster simply left in a huff? Instead, he had let himself be embarrassed in front of a crowd—embarrassed so badly, in fact, that he flew into a rage and tried to destroy everyone.

Oh, well, it didn't matter now. Nothing mattered. A vision of day after day of brown rice and broccoli marched through his mind. Feather and his stomach both sighed.

At least the giant, awful machine was in ruins. Kokopelli wouldn't be flinging pies anytime soon.

"That's what *you* think!" chuckled the Muse of Tricks in his best—or was it his worst?—mind-reading mode. "I can always do it the old-fashioned way!" A fresh little banana cream pie had somehow appeared in Kokopelli's hand. How did he *do* that?

"Not if I pie you first!" bellowed Chad. Feather noted without any particular interest that Chad also seemed to be armed with a pie, a beautifully browned pumpkin pie still steaming from the oven. Chad quick-pitched it, without warning or windup, straight at Kokopelli's head. The trickster ducked. The pie sailed past him and pasted itself squarely on the end of Pwt's nose.

"Hfgh!" coughed Pwt. He, too, had a pie. After a pause to scoop the pumpkin custard off his face, he fired back at Chad. With a *plurff,* Chad was suddenly coated with a brilliant yellow, jellylike material studded with nuggets of creamy white topping. Lemon meringue, thought Feather gloomily. So what.

As Aeiou poured a glass of synthetic prune juice over Chad's head, Feather suddenly remembered the moment when Kokopelli had agreed to talk. It was just after he had looked through the telescope. Why? The question gnawed at Feather's brain like a persistent beaver gnawing an especially tough stump.

"Urania," he asked, over a background clatter of falling pie tins, "what made Kokopelli so willing to talk after he looked through the telescope last night? Why did seeing the rings of Saturn make him so cooperative?"

Urania dodged a glistening strawberry-rhubarb pie, which came to rest on Bo's hindquarters. The cow lowered her horns and began chasing Kokopelli around the room.

"Saturn? That wasn't Saturn."

"It wasn't?"

"Look for yourself."

Feather again stepped to the telescope and peered through the eyepiece. It certainly looked like Saturn. There were the great rings once again. Odd, he thought, to see it in broad daylight. He turned and looked quizzically at Urania.

Urania pointed to the top of the telescope. Feather looked up. His stomach came back to life with a roar like a Bengal tiger on a hunger strike. The sound stopped Bo in her tracks. She reversed direction and began fleeing from Kokopelli.

There, in midair, hung a doughnut. It dangled by a string from a fishing pole tied to the telescope barrel with several windings of stout rope. The doughnut itself hovered just beyond the end of the telescope. Anyone looking would see the pastry magnified to immense proportions. That was no doughnut-shaped astronomical object he had seen; it was a REAL DOUGHNUT! And not just any doughnut, either, but a glistening Krusty-Glop single-glazed maple old-fashioned, his favorite. Even from this distance he recognized it. His heart began to beat a wild rock-'n'-roll rhythm.

"When Kokopelli looked through the telescope and saw that doughnut," explained Urania, "he knew he had lost. I had doughnuts to give you, whereas he never meant to give you a thing. In fact, he ate them all himself. So now, he saw, you would be helping me instead of him. The poor little Muse of Tricks realized he had lost the power to aim his machine. And that's when he agreed to talk."

"Wait a minute," Feather interrupted eagerly. "Did you say *doughnuts,* with an *s?*"

"I did, and they're all yours. But you'd better hurry. It's getting pretty sticky down here."

"Thank you, Urania, thank you!" cried Feather, and without another microsecond's delay, he scampered up the telescope. He found a firm foothold in the sticky dollops of pie that encrusted the lower parts of the instrument, but even then his own agility amazed him. His mind was so focused, his limbs so coordinated, his appetite so eager, he barely noticed when a strawberry-rhubarb pie winged his elbow and ricocheted off into Aeiou, who was busily tossing glasses of synthetic prune juice in all directions.

At the top, Feather arranged himself in a comfortable squat and reached for the doughnut. This time, no one snatched it away. He raised it to his beak, closed his eyes, and breathed deeply. The perfume was heavenly! He savored it for ages. When at last he opened his eyes again, he noticed a little shelf nestled against the wall. On the shelf was a long, narrow box with the Krusty-Glop logo printed on its lid. He opened it. There were a dozen doughnuts—not old and cold, but fresh and warm, a brand-new box provided by Urania and the rest.

Down below, pies were still flying. Droplets of juice splashed up at him, and bits of whipped cream, custard, fruit, and meringue dotted his coat and his feathers. He looked down at a sticky mosaic of wild colors. It was so beautiful. Somewhere, far away, Muses were shrieking. Was that laughter he heard? Feather took a bite of his doughnut. A glorious, warm sensation flooded his body, spreading from the tip of his tongue all the way to his fingers and toes. The wild beast inside him quit growling.

At last. Everything was right with the world—wasn't it?